BREAKING LOOP-II
(KARANJIOSLAMAN- IN QUEST OF HEART)

AF121035

MASTER IVAYAAN

BLUEROSE PUBLISHERS
India | U.K.

Copyright © Master Ivayaan 2024

All rights reserved by author. No part of this publication may be reproduced, stored in a retrieval system or transmitted in any form or by any means, electronic, mechanical, photocopying, recording or otherwise, without the prior permission of the author. Although every precaution has been taken to verify the accuracy of the information contained herein, the publisher assumes no responsibility for any errors or omissions. No liability is assumed for damages that may result from the use of information contained within.

BlueRose Publishers takes no responsibility for any damages, losses, or liabilities that may arise from the use or misuse of the information, products, or services provided in this publication.

For permissions requests or inquiries regarding this publication, please contact:

BLUEROSE PUBLISHERS
www.BlueRoseONE.com
info@bluerosepublishers.com
+91 8882 898 898
+4407342408967

ISBN: 978-93-6452-616-6

Cover Design: Vishal Jha
Typesetting: Pooja Sharma

First Edition: August 2024

DEDICATION

To my parents, Susmita Das and Niranjan Pattnaik, who moulded me into a better person and inspired me to write.

ACKNOWLEDGEMENTS

My first debt is to my aunt, Pratima Das Mohanty;my uncle Ranjit Kumar Mohanty; and my sister, Varsha Mohanty, who spared their valuable time to help me in the conception of this book. I would also want to thank Vishal Jha; The owner of Artflix studios who had put immense effort into making the cover design of this book… He listened to all my babbles and kept on changing and doing work without any complaints. truly indebted to you. Thank you for your hardwork and effort.

PREFACE

Every human has a good and bad side, some parts of the devil and some parts of the angel both reside in a human. It depends on the human's fascination which side he choses to explore. A person who explores its devil parts and deepens its roots is called a sinner meanwhile a person who explores its angelic side and deepens its root is known to be heavenly person. Both are not much different, they just happen to support different opinions which according to the human rules have been set to two sides; wrong and right. Similarly a human who is a sinner and had done heinous crimes should not be given a easy death and that's not only in the case of humans rather the gods of every religion do say so according to our scriptures, but many a times we fail to understand the situation as to why the person had to choose the path for which he is to be punished, may be we can give him/her a second chance to live his/her life again with different circumstances than his/her previous one and then we can lead to the conclusion if that person is a sinner or innocent. If the person choses its devilish side in both his life with two different options then only can they be judged. From the day humans have taken birth, the story of revenge and war has been common, which shows how humans keep licking their pasts without even trying to move on from it, like in a war they try to point out the reason who tried to start the war first rather than thinking of ending it they keep blaming each other and warring. Just like if two person; person A and person B are having a peaceful conversation and suddenly due to a wrong talk or miscommunication A hits B and in return B replies with a hit back. After sometime when they get tired they start to discuss who started the fight without realizing that they both were kind of responsible for the start, as there must be a reason why A hit B and there must be a reason why B had to state the fact that angered A to a point of hitting B. They keep arguing over the reason and in turn lose the conscience and start behaving like animals without logical thoughts and behavior, thus starting the chain of revenge. Someone needs to step up and break the chain meanwhile the other should accept it so as to stop the bloodshed. This is the harsh reality of humans; They never accept their mistakes.

This is a work of pure fiction but it may happen in the future or may have happened in the past. There are many secrets in the world that is yet to be unraveled.

The movies I have seen and the books I have read inspired me to develop such a universe, or more specifically the multiverse; THE MULTIVERSE OF THE SUPREME.

SUMMARY

After the curse tale's curse got wiped out from Earth-7 and the devil promised to wipe out the existence of Aiden from the timeline to protect humanity, Aiden was reborn. The devil broke his promise as he wanted Aiden to live a life that will teach him the true meaning of sacrifice and the value of a human life. Thus the devil put him in another body and let Aiden live the life of another person. Now Aiden has to lead a knew life that he is totally unaware of, and the solve the mysteries of the new life finally leading him to learn the new secrets of a new life on a new world. Can he overcome the problems and find the paving stone to build a new life for himself or he would be trapped again a loop of life games and end up losing to the devil again? Will he be able to clear out the threats or ignore it to hide and lead a life of his own? Let's come back to the adventures of Aiden and explore the new mysteries and secrets that the new life is going to unveil for him.

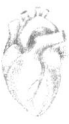

CONTENTS

1. WHAT THE HELL 4
2. IN SEARCH OF 12
3. CONFUSION 21
4. OPPOSITE 28
5. DECAPITATED CHANCE 35
6. STARTS AGAIN 43
7. DON'T RETURN TO 50
8. BLOOD VERSUS POISON 58
9. RUN, KILL, RUN 69
10. AIDEN? 80
11. OBSESSION OR INSANITY? 89
12. THE DEATH BOUNDARY 98
13. KARAN 105
14. KARANJIOSLAMAN 113
15. MISSION 124
16. MIND FIGHT 132
17. CHOSEN LIFE 142
18. THE LOOP 151
19. SECRETS 158

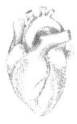

THE END?

Lucifer came to Earth to meet his father. His father had taken human form and was born as a human child. He is now 14 years old, but has all his memories. He met Lucifer and talked to him. Lucifer was still confused about Aiden as neither could he get a life of his own nor was he punished for his sins. God smiled and said, "You are the leader of that universe and have complete authority to decide how his life proceeds, but remember you had already wiped out his existence from the timeline of that universe and if you try to insert it forcefully, there will be a distortion in nature's law. Besides, the curse will be re-imposed, wiping out all humans from the face of the Earth. Do something that would work without distorting natural laws or killing people. Wiping out Aiden's existence was not a good idea as he was redeemed of his sins without realising them. Besides, you are also attached to that boy and want him to have a life of his own."

After listening to all this, Lucifer smiled that his father understood him and he was happy that his reviving Aiden idea was not a mistake. Now, How to revive him was a major problem. He searched for ideas to revive Aiden and let him realise the pain he had caused to thousands of people because God, angels, demons or humans everyone should realise their mistakes and should face the consequences of it, beside that he also wanted him to lead a life which he lost two times on this earth. So Lucifer started consulting with other gods, and after much discussions Lucifer retracted Aiden's memory and traced it over the memories of another person in another universe that followed a completely different timeline. He decided to give Aiden another opportunity to live his life as a human and will be punished or rewarded according to the deeds done by him in his new life.

Lucifer looked at all the possibilities of that person's life whose memories and consciousness would be retraced by Aiden's. He checked his past, present and future, realising it would be the perfect life and punishment for Aiden. He also realised that after putting Aiden in that Human's body there would be many possibilities of how he would end up, but one possibility really seemed distorted; he could not recognise the occurrence of the possibility because of some interference of a higher being, more powerful than any angel or god, more powerful than himself.

Thinking that the possibility had a minimal probability of occurrence, he ignored it and implemented Aiden's punishment. The person into whom Aiden's memories were traced, that person brain would not remember his own past, his family, or anything that would help him to revive himself, that person would lose somewhere inside that body. Aiden would live a life where he be running errands, finding his own existence.

Aiden would also remember the deaths of people from his previous world, the memory of the curse, he would remember every death, the tears of people and yet he won't be able to change it.. However, this was not the only punishment; doomsday was about to fall. Would Aiden be able to escape his fate?

Lucifer, realising that Aiden was not the only one responsible for the deaths of those people from the curse, went into the death pain room in hell where the pain of all those who had died and the agony of their loved and dear ones can be felt by him. Lucifer told Satan to lock the door and not open it even if he heard him screaming. Satan was to release him only when Aiden broke the loop. The loop that would continue till the end of universe, until and unless Aiden finds his way out of it.

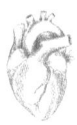

Chapter 1

WHAT THE HELL....

Aiden was racing down the busy road as if escaping from someone. The whole city was in chaos; accidents were happening, fires had started at many places, ambulances and fire brigades were rushing about. Aiden kept running until he reached a hospital. He entered it, drank some water, sat down, and calmed down. He was not sure what was happening. He saw many patients being brought as if the accidents did not seem to end.

Aiden was huffing and suddenly he saw some persons behind him. He got frightened and started running again. He ran upstairs, but stopped midway when he saw a storeroom under the stairs. He jumped from the stairs and entered it. He started thinking why he was panicking so much. Even though he had never come here earlier, the place felt somewhat familiar to him.

He wondered who those men were whom he was scared of; he did not know them. As soon as he had seen them, his instinct screamed to him to run far from them. His heart was pounding so hard that he could hear it even in so much chaos. He was sweating all over. There was a knock on the door. Slowly, its sound and frequency increased. Aiden did not know what to do.

He put on a doctor's gown and a surgical mask and opened the door with trepidation. Three men grabbed him and took him to the operation theatre. He was shocked to see what was happening with him. He was terrified

That they would dissect him to experiment. He was powerless; his muscles became numb, he realised he could not move his body even an inch, he couldn't free himself from their grasps. Finally, he decided to accept his fate.

One of the nurses called out to him, "Doctor, there is a severe accident case. A girl has lost a lot of blood and you have to treat her urgently." Aiden was confused as to whom the nurse was referring as doctor and who was this girl for whom they were so tensed. The injured girl was brought in on a stretcher. Seeing her raised goose bumps on him. Half her body was churned exposing her internal organs and blood kept oozing out.

Aiden was shocked to see the extent of her injuries; luckily, she was still breathing. She caught his hand and spoke faintly, "Help me." A tear flowed down Aiden's cheek. He did not know why he felt such sympathy for a stranger. The nurse told him to start treatment immediately. He did not want to be responsible for anyone's death, so he just removed his mask and told them he was not a doctor but had to take up the doctor's get up to hide from some people.

All his talks were of no avail as the timeline was repeated in front of him. As he was standing there the nurses and the injured girl faded away. The same people who carried him into the operation theatre were now seen carrying another man into the operation theatre. The severely injured girl was bought again into the room by the nurses and the nurses started pleading the man to treat the girl. This time the man who was bought in wore a surgical mask and the was treated by a genuine doctor. Aiden kept staring without understanding what was going on.

He tried to run away but saw that the door had been reduced to the size of a post box slot. He froze where he stood with his face showing a mixture of many expressions. His emotions were confused. He was not sure if he was scared, sad, or angry. He looked on while the operation was being done. This time he saw that the doctor is pealing the skin, muscles, and tissues of the nurses and grafting them on the girl's body. She was silent while the nurses screamed in pain. Even though Aiden could not watch the scene, his body did not let him close his eyes, it was as if he was being forced to watch the gruesome scenery, he tried to close his eyes but it felt as if he had lost his eyelids.

He kept staring at the scene. After an hour or two, the operation ended. Suddenly Aiden's eyes blinked and he was happy to regain his reflexes. After another blink he saw that all the nurses were all right. The doctor had disappeared. They came to Aiden and congratulated him for a successful operation. Aiden could not say anything. He was struck dumb.

Before he could realise what was happening, he saw the girl remove the saline needles pierced into her nerves, removed the oxygen mask from he face and walked towards the nurses. She stood near them staring at them for some moment and then suddenly pounced on one and started ripping her flesh and eating it. One by one she fed on the other nurses too and like a cannibal. The more she fed on them, the more her injuries were healing. The stitches were becoming a part of her body, her cut up body parts were regenrating. She looked towards Aiden and gestured, "You are the last tasty treat."

Aiden was scared, he ran towards the door that had shrunk but was amazed to find that he could squeeze through. He ran towards the exit from where he entered the hospital initially but could not find it. He was trapped in a maze. He ran towards the stairs. He stopped at some distance from the operation theatre to get his breath back but looked back to see the girl coming towards him with her eyes indicating she was lusting for his blood. Without wasting another minute Aiden ran upstairs and took a sharp left turn. He was astonished to see the hospital was completely empty. It was like a no-man's land. He was shocked that, some time ago there were hundreds of doctors and nurse treating thousands of patients and suddenly it was empty as if ghosted by some unknown force. Luckily, he saw a man and begged him for his help.

But before the man could take any action, the girl jumped on the man and started feeding on him. Aiden saw all this cruelty and realised that the more he asked for help, the more people were going to die. He kept running from floor to floor until he reached the terrace. He looked down and saw there was no way to escape. He was already on the 24th floor. If he jumped down from there, he would surely die. If he remained where he was, he would be eaten by the girl till death. Now he had two option either to die a sudden death by jumping off from the roof or die gradually being eaten by the mindless cannibal. He chose a sudden and less painful death, rather than a painful one. He jumped off the terrace and closed his eyes. After some time, he realised he there was no gush of wind rushing against him, he opened his eyes and was awestruck to see that he was standing on the ground floor of the hospital.

He looked around and saw the girl running downstairs, her eyes fixated on him. Aiden was standing near the door, the exit door and as he was about to open it, a truck carrying iron rods crashed in and a rod pierced his chest and came out of his back with his heart stuck to it, still beating. Aiden half suspended in the air tried to look back but his body had lost its energy, he looked into the truck's side mirror and saw the girl rushing towards him.

As soon as the girl pounced on him Aiden woke up from his unnaturally long dream and looked around. His face was blank. He looked around while still lying on the bed. He was confused for some time and then suddenly realised he should have been dead. To be more accurate, his very existence should have been wiped out.

He jumped out of bed and looked out of the window. There was no one on the streets. He thought everyone had been wiped out; this thought did not affect his emotions. He was very calm and composed. He tried shouting; to feel the agony and pain but nothing happened.

Just then, the door of his room burst open and an old man dressed as a butler came with three or four bodyguards, he was so distressed and distracted that he was unable to count the number of men rushing in. Calling Aiden 'Master', the butler asked, "Are you all right, Sir?" Aiden looked at them and noticed that the room, the place, the people all were stranger. He did not recognise anything or anyone. He stared at them for some time and in a trembling voice asked who they were.

The butler asked, "Sir, did you see one of those ugly dreams again? I am your butler working for you for the last fifty-two years." Aiden raised his eyebrows thinking he was still dreaming. He hit himself in an attempt to bring himself to reality. The butler tried to stop him but Aiden ordered him not to interfere. He kept hitting himself until he fell down unconscious. After some time, he came to his senses and seeing himself at the same place surrounded by same people he realised that it was not a dream and he was very much alive as any other human present in that room. "The devil hadn't kept his word"This thought struck his mind, but these thoughts can be kept for some other day for now he has to think of the situation he was in; surrounded by tensed looking strangers, staring at him.

Aiden realised he is trapped in something he could not understand. He looked carefully at all of them and felt he could trust only the butler. He whispered into his ears to tell the others to leave. The butler laughed, "You are our Master; you can directly order anyone to leave or stay."

Aiden ordered everyone except the butler to leave the room. He looked tensed and pale but only by looks as on the inside he felt hollow. Aiden asked him very politely where he was and who they were. There were more questions whirling in his mind so he asked the butler . he asked if it was a plan of Lucifer to let him believe he was having a normal life and then would give him a tragic jolt that would dump him into a pit full of sadness, the butler stood there silently staring at his master not knowing what to answer. Aiden went on blabbering that this might be one of the hell loops prepared by Deimos, the assistant of Lucifer, who creates hell loops from people's imagination so that they could be trapped and punished for their sins.

He started screaming Lucifer's name and ran to the door, opened it and rushed downstairs, looked here and there but only he could find was the workers, the chef, and the drivers. He went up to one of the workers and asked if he had seen Lucifer. After his denial, he pleaded with the other workers saying it was all Lucifer's fault and not his mistake.

The workers looked at him, totally shocked. He walked up to the butler and whispered in his ears, "He has gone insane." The butler nodded in agreement but did not know what to do. Seeing him pleading with some of the other workers, the butler rushed to him repeating, "Master, Master, Master, listen to me...." At last, he could take it no more and shouted his name, "Karan."

Aiden was taken aback, surprised and many more emotions came as thoughts to his mind but he couldn't feel it. He looked at the butler who was looking at him while calling out the name Karan and asked who Karan was. The butler was really frustrated , he could take this madness no more so he just told him to find out on his own. Realising that it was only this 'Karan' who could save him, Aiden decided to find him but before leaving in search of his only hope he wanted to have some food, he felt hungry as if he had not had any food from centuries. He asked the butler for some food and the butler took him to the dining room where the table was decorated with lots of varieties of food The table was lined with turkey, chicken different varieties of rice, buns and roti. There were salad, desserts and many more. He was mesmerised by its aroma. He couldn't decide what to have so he decided to eat a little from every dish. After a proper meal, he got up and got ready to go in search of Karan. He went into the room the butler signalled to get dressed but was astonished to see girls standing on both sides of the corridor.

Aiden asked them to introduce themselves. One by one the girls introduced themselves and told him that they were Aiden's personal dressers.

Aiden realised that he was an extremely rich person just as he wanted his life to be. He was now sure that this was Lucifer's handiwork. He had tried every method to meet him but they were of no avail. So, he went in search for Karan.

First, he needed some material to start his search. He went to his butler and asked if he had any photo of Karan or whether he could tell him anything to help him find him. The butler looked at him, but could not say anything because he was loyal to his master. He went into the room and brought a photo of Karan which he gave him. Aiden looked at it and asked him if he was sure that this person could help him. The butler nodded.

Aiden took the bike key and left in search of Karan. The helper asked the butler why he did not he just tell him the truth. The butler replied, "The greatest therapy is self-help therapy, a person depressed, sad or confused can clear all this only with his own help by kicking out the doubts and madness he/she holds about themselves. The level of insanity that Master is showing is not normal. Therefore, he needs to find the truth on his own. Only then will he realise his mistake and the insanity he is showing."

The helper smiled and nodded. Aiden looked determined to find Karan and get out of the hell loop he was trapped in. The only thing that confused him was why had Lucifer revived him and even if he hadn't and this is one of his hell loop then why is he leading such an ideal life? Even with all these questions swirling in his mind Aiden felt empty; he was devoid of the most important thing in human life.

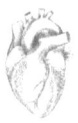

Chapter 2

IN SEARCH OF....

Aiden looked around his surroundings and all seemed like a real world. For a moment, he started to feel that it was the real world and that he was still alive, but then he shook his head and told himself, "The Devil deceives." He kept on going, showing people Karan's photo and asking if they know where to find him. The first person just ignored him; the second one told him to go to a psychiatrist while the third slapped him. The fourth one simply refused to answer while the fifth told him to ask someone else. The sixth was not interested in his question.

As he went further, he saw a crowd on the roadside. Being curious to know why such a huge crowd had gathered, he parked his bike on the side of the road and walked up to them. He asked the people what had happened there but no one replied. They were busy; some trying to call an ambulance some were clicking photos and videos while others were trying to get the victim's contact number to inform friends and family.

Aiden got a glimpse of the victim and his eyes widened. He pushed deeper into the crowd. At last, he got to get a clear view of the victim. His eyes started to get wet. He rushed to pick up the girl, but as soon as he reached the girl, her eyes opened and she stared at him. She was bleeding caused by the severe accident she had been involved in. Aiden wasn't shocked due to her being alive despite her injuries rather what was more shocking was she was the girl that Aiden dreamed about the other day. She woke up, supporting her back against the scooter behind her, sat beside Aiden, still bleeding, and touched his forehead. Suddenly Aiden fell into a pit of darkness

He remembered a similar experience and cursed Lucifer for giving him the power to know someone's past by just touching them. The Devil had given him that power to remember his past and initiate the curse in his previous life. He recalled that even after being to hell, even after feeling sorry and even after his existence being wiped out he still had that power in him. He looked around in that pitch dark pit and saw a ray of light. He ran towards it and came to a cheerful place where children were playing but all those children were kind of blurred out and among them one child glowed like the sun.

Aiden realised that it was the childhood of the same injured girl who touched his forehead some time ago. Aiden focused on the scenery in front of him, He saw while she was playing with her friends, someone came running towards her, grabbed her, and pushed her into a van. The van drove away. Aiden looked at all this without any intention to follow it. That was when he realised he was not what he used to be. The earlier Aiden would have rushed behind the van to rescue the girl. He thought that this change was nothing serious and it may be due to the fact that he had become habituated to the power and his subconscious mind knew that this is someone else thoughts. And so, even if he tried to rush and save the girl, he could not. However, as he was inside the girl's memory, he was teleported to the place where she had been taken to. He saw her enjoying herself with the man who had kidnapped her. Aiden went closer to the window to watch both of them play inside that tiny house, both of them were happy and were playing hide and seek.

Aiden did not show any expression but as he advanced into the house his eyes widened. He kept staring at the girl and the man. The man turned his head and Aiden realised that he was the one whom he was searching for, the one for whom people slapped him and called him a madman. He was none other than Karan. Aiden recognised him as soon as he saw him, but as he tried to approach him, Karan vanished and the girl caught hold of Aiden's hand. While holding his hand she cried excitedly "I found you, I found you". He tried to free himself but while doing so tripped and fell. He opened his eyes and looked around him. He was out into the real world again. The people at the accident site were staring at him with anger in their eyes. One of them asked if he knew the girl.

Aiden looked down and realised the question had been asked because he was holding the girl's hand. He did not know what to reply so he just nodded his head and said he was her lover. He carried her in his arms and told one of the bystanders to start his car. He hesitated as he did not want any blood in his car and feared he might be interrogated by the police, but Aiden gave him a deadly glance that made him relent. He was still afraid so he just gave him his car key.

Aiden laid the girl down on the back seat and drove the car to the nearest hospital. Just as he left and the crowd started to disperse, an ambulance arrived. They were informed about the situation what and the ambulance driver immediately contacted the police. After reaching the nearest hospital, Aiden recognised that it was the same hospital from his dream. The girl was taken into the operation theatre while Aiden filled out a form as her legal guardian. All this time he wanted to fear the fact that his dream might come true and the girl may start feeding on the people, but keeping his fears aside he stayed there and proceeded to do the payment. He did not know how to make the payment and then remembered he had a phone whose password he typed subconsciously as if someone else was controlling his hand.

He saw his call log that showed calls to a particular number that had been saved as 'Vaahindi'. Aiden called that number and discovered it was the butler's name. He wanted to laugh, but couldn't. He just told the butler to bring an amount of four lakhs as it was an emergency. The butler agreed and in a short period some men came with the money and gave it to Aiden. He deposited it in the account section and submitted the form. The operation started.

Aiden sat there outside the operation theatre thinking about the relationship between the girl and Karan. He could not figure it out. He thought If this wasn't hell then what is, and if this really is his hell loop then why is he given a mystery to solve rather than experiencing his own miseries again and again. It was a hell lot of a confusion for him . The day he wakes up from the nightmare, he meets the girl he had seen in it and she turns out to be connected to the person he is looking for. He did not know what to do. He wanted to get frustrated but couldn't. He felt very incomplete as if something was missing in him.

All these thoughts made him wonder whether this could be the real world. However, according to the deal with the Devil he was not supposed to be reborn and the world would be free of the curse. Then he remembered that Lucifer had made everyone forget that the curse or Aiden had ever existed. This may have had an adverse effect and made people think that the deaths that were taking place were due to the natural causes when they were actually due to the curse.

Aiden was confused over what to do. Whether to find Karan first who is the only one who could help him or return to his homeland to know if the curse has been stopped or not. he was crushed by the weight of his thoughts which were suddenly interrupted by the entry of the police. They had come to investigate the accident. Without wasting a moment they started interrogating. "So, what is your name?" Aiden replied. The constable was noting down everything. "So, Aiden, tell us about the accident."

He looked directly at them and said he had not seen it. He happened to be nearby and had just seen the injured girl before rushing her to the hospital. The police then asked whether or not he had told the people at the accident site that he was her lover and had also filled the hospital form as her local guardian. Aiden nodded and the police asked in a sarcastic tone "So would you care to tell me her name, a coincidentally present lover?"

Aiden took a deep breath. He wanted to tell them that he had seen the girl for the second time. In the first time, she had thirsted for his blood and wanted to kill him, but he paused for a second and realised how stupid that would be for them to hear such a story, so instead he told them that He did not know much about her because they had not talked for long, so he doesn't know her name. The police after hearing this gave him a cold look, and suddenly he uttered what struck him, "Sihira." The police verified it and it seemed that Aiden was speaking the truth as it happened to be her name. The inspector was about to interrogate further when he received a call to be present at the police station immediately.

Two constables stayed there while the inspector went away after strictly instructing them not to allow anyone to see the girl. He had to be informed as soon as she recovered.

After an hour or two the doctor came out of the operation theatre. He told Aiden nothing could be concluded until the girl regained consciousness. Till then, she would remain under medical observation 24 x 7. He had stitched the wounds; the bleeding had stopped and now all depended on how her body reacts. "So, let's hope for the best."

Aiden decided to stay there as she was the only one who knew Karan. The girl was taken out of the operation theatre and taken to the general ward. He tried to go meet her but the constables stopped him. He had no choice but to wait outside. He ate and slept in the hospital or acted as if he was sleeping. He was waiting for the moment when the constables would fall asleep and then he could visit her. He acted till midnight when he heard deep breathes of the constables. He woke up and slowly tiptoed into Sihira's ward. He touched her again and again trying to travel into her memories but nothing worked. This went on for three days; everyday he would tiptoe into her ward trying to jump into her thoughts to learn more about Karan but he couldn't. On the fourth day, the doctor gave him some good news about Sihira's health. He said her vitals were showing good signs of development and she might regain consciousness any time now. Aiden just nodded. The constables realising she might be gaining her consciousness anytime now guarded the entrance more carefully.

In the evening the doctor and nurses rushed into Sihira's ward closing the door behind them. Aiden and the constables got tensed as to what may be the emergency. The doctor came out after sometime informing them that there is nothing to worry as the girl has gained her consciousness and she would recover soon. As soon as Aiden came to know about it, he tried to rush in , but was stopped by the constables. They contacted the inspector and after half an hour or so the inspector arrived and went in to meet the girl. The doctor warned him that the girl was physically hurt and mentally disturbed so she should not be pressurised or her condition could worsen. The inspector assured him that he would only ask some general questions to clear his doubts. The inspector started questioning the girl.

"So, Sihira, right?" She nodded in agreement. She had still not recovered fully so she was in no condition to understand all the questions properly. The inspector questioned further, "So, you remember everything about the accident?" She agreed again. "Who saved you?" The inspector asked this to merely check if she truly remembered everything. Sihira spoke but due to her injuries she couldn't speak properly, her words were not audible. The inspector went close to her to hear the words clearly and he heard the name.

He was surprised and said, "But ma'am, a boy named Aiden saved you who claims to be your lover. He had filled the hospital form as your legal guardian." Sihira shook her head in disagreement. The inspector called in Aiden to confirm but Sihira couldn't stay awake any longer and fell asleep. The inspector tried to wake her up but Aiden stopped him and asked him what she had said. The inspector knew he could no longer believe Aiden so he just said that she was not in a good condition to say anything worthwhile.

He went away and again warning his constables not to allow anyone into the ward and to keep an eye on Aiden. They brought Aiden out of the ward. Aiden sat outside.

Just then his phone rang. It was Vaahindi, his butler. He told Aiden to return home as he had not come for three days. After reaching home, Aiden told Vaahindi that his wallet did not have his driving licence and other necessary documents. Vaahindi told him that some days ago his wallet was stolen. A complaint had been made and the xerox copies were in his cupboard. Aiden was too tired to look for them. He had his food and went off to sleep immediately afterwards. At 3 in the night, the inspector called to inform him that the girl had regained consciousness.

Half asleep Aiden rushed to the hospital where the inspector asked the girl to identify if he was the one who had saved her. The girl slowly caught Aiden's hands and murmured the name again, before relapsing into unconsciousness. Aiden was confused for some moments. He realised something and ran to the washroom and was shocked to see himself in the mirror. All these days he had been looking here and there and in all this hectic schedule he never got a chance to look into the mirror and if he had looked once he wouldn't have to wander here and there like a madmen. He himself was Karan, the man he was looking for, somehow he was residing in Karan's body, a fine toned man with a clean face and jawline way too good, he was so good looking that he gave a Godly complexion, he was no less handsome than Lucifer himself. Aiden kept staring at the mirror for some moment without knowing about the handsome face, Aiden was speechless. Slowly the pieces started joining together in his head.

The butler calling him Karan, people slapping and ignoring him, the girl calling out to him, his nightmare all the pieces of the jigsaw puzzle that led to Karan, in whose body he was currently in all this came together in his head. He was confused over what was going on. Now he was sure that he was not in hell as in hell a person's memory were tortured in their original body and not in someone else's. However, there were still many questions to be answered. Where was he? Who was Karan and why was he in his body. And the most important question was why is he alive?

Chapter 3

CONFUSION....

Aiden thought of going home and ask Vaahindi what was going on but as soon as he stepped out of the washroom, the constables caught him and the inspector told them to take him to the police station. Aiden knew why he was being arrested so he did not resist but just went along with them to the station. There, Aiden tried to call his butler but the constables seized his phone and hung up the call. Seeing his Master's missed call the butler called him back. One of the constables answered and told him about how Karan had filled the hospital form with a fake name and thus they have been ordered to jail him until the inspector arrived.

The butler called the lawyer, informed him of the situation and told him to apply for bail. The inspector arrived at the station and started interrogating Aiden, "Why did you lie?" Aiden knew they would not believe him so he remained silent. The inspector kept questioning him but got no answers. He was frustrated seeing Aiden so calm and composed. He told Aiden to look at him and answer his questions.

Aiden did so looked into the inspector's eyes but without a trace of fear in his eyes. The inspector punched him in the face, grabbed his collar, and told him to spit out the truth or he would beat him to death. The inspector doubted whether he was truly the girl's boyfriend or was trying to do something to the girl. Aiden could see the anger raging in the inspector's eyes but he was confused as to what to answer. Any truth he said would only prove him insane.

Since Aiden had nothing to say, he looked at him and said his lawyer would speak to him and that any action against him without any evidence would be illegal. These words were like pouring oil in fire. The inspector enraged was about to hit him again but was stopped by his constables at the last moment. He went into his cabin. Aiden sat there calm and silent looking at the floor. He was not feeling anything so he thought it would be better not to make any eye contact with anyone.

The inspector's doubt had increased seeing Aiden's expressionless face. He seemed unmoved even after his lover was involved in such a severe accident. He did not shed a tear. The inspector was deep in thought and fell asleep on the table as he was very tired. Aiden leaned against the wall and closed his eyes remembering his mother and girlfriend for whom he had sacrificed his own life. He started thinking how peaceful a life they would be leading now as he was not with them anymore.

Just then he realised that he was still alive and that the curse might have killed them. He asked the constable in which place he was now. The constable looked at him, irritated by his question replied in a rather sarcastic manner that he was now at his wedding. Aiden pointed out it was a serious matter, saying this he grabbed the inspector's hand and fell into a dark pit again, but couldn't stay there longer as the constable pulled away his hand. The constable realised that Aiden could be mentally unstable and told him he is at the police station. The constable then rushed into the inspector's cabin to tell him his theory.

Aiden wanted to ask which country and which state they were in now but the constable misinterpreted it and before Aiden could ask his question the constable had already left for the inspector's cabin after instructing another constable to keep an eye on Aiden. Aiden was impatient and continuously stamped his legs and tapped his fingers. He could wait no more and stood up and asked the second constable in which country he was in now. The constable was confused and replied they were in Milatintia. Aiden gave him an interrogative look. The constable just nodded his head in agreement.

Aiden sat down and kept imagining what could have happened. Sometimes he thought that one of the policemen was Lucifer but ruled it out. Then again he thought, "If the inspector is the Devil then he knew I would find him easily so one of the lower ranked officials must be him." He went to the constable guarding him and asked him if everyone at Lihamantos was well or not; this constable, like the earlier one, also got confused.

Aiden sighed and told him he would accept any punishment, but he needed to know if the Devil had kept his side of the deal and that his family was safe and leading a happy life. The constable was silent for a long time but Aiden's constant nagging irritated him so much that he brought a pair of handcuffs and cuffed Aiden to the chair he was sitting on. It had no effect, as after remaining silent for a while, Aiden started blabbering again. He said the punishment he was getting was not part of the deal. The constable shouted at him and ran into the inspector's cabin to inform his senior constable and told the inspector about the crazy things Aiden is talking about.

The inspector listened patiently. He realised that the constable's theory might be correct and Aiden might have developed a multiple personality disorder. They knew nothing of his past or the traumas that might have led to his present condition. The inspector tried talking to him again, this time with a more calm and sensitive mind.

Aiden had fallen asleep. The inspector sprinkled some water on his face and woke him up. He asked him about his past. Aiden stared at him for some time and then smiled. The inspector was confused and asked why he was smiling. Aiden burst into laughter and told him to stop acting. "So you knew that I would think you will become one of the low ranking officers so as to confuse me and let me think whether you resided in the inspector's body or not. You may not be residing in someone else body rather you took the form of a human and work here as an inspector so as to keep a close look on me.'

The inspector was on the verge of crying, he was really frustrated from all this crap he has been hearing. He gave him some water and told him to calm down. Aiden kept repeating to him not to act. After a certain period, the inspector was at his wits end and told him he could not escape prison by acting crazy. Aiden raised his eyebrows and realised he had come back from where he had started and that none of them is the devil.

He went into the world of imagination again and became silent. The inspector got tired of asking questions and went into his cabin. He did not know what to do. He told the constable to call a psychiatrist for help and ordered them to constantly keep an eye on Aiden.

Just then, Vaahindi came in with a lawyer and slammed the bail order on the inspector's table who told the constable to remove Aiden's handcuffs. The lawyer told Vaahindi to take Aiden with him. All this happened so quickly that the inspector did not know how to react. He just sat there staring at the bail order. After some minutes, he picked it up and placed it in a file. He called the constable and told him to bring a detailed report on the man named Karan within two days.

Vaahindi was quiet all along the ride but as soon as they reached home Vaahindi asked Aiden why he was acting so weirdly. Aiden's eyes opened wide. He grabbed the butler and said, "Now I realise that you are the Devil, someone who can always stay with a person is a butler. You have taken on the appearance of a butler." The butler was confused asked if he had mistaken him for someone else.

Aiden shook his hands in desperation and realised he was going crazy. The butler asked him, "You had promised that you wouldn't meet that girl again and yet you went to her aid and also stayed by her side day and night to protect her. See what she has done to you. You have gone mad." Aiden realised that this man Karan had some past link with the girl named Sihira. He thought of asking about her but realised that the more the people came to know, the more they will think he has gone mad. He decided to remain silent and make plans to move out of there.

He tried to find his identity cards. The butler gave him the Xerox ones. Aiden looked at the duplicates of the identity cards of Karan, the man in whose body he was at the moment. He couldn't find anything useful in those identities except for date of birth, address, and parents' name. Karan is a 28-year-old businessman and one of the richest persons in the country. He told the butler that even after having everything, he felt something important missing in his life. The butler smiled and replied, "That's the eternal truth of humans, Sir!"

Aiden asked him the meaning of those words. The butler explained "Humans always keep complaining about what they miss. They never praise the things they have. They are never satisfied; they always want more and more and in the end that 'more' goes to such an extent that a human can't take it anymore and their life shatters, just like a kid who keeps on blowing into a balloon in the hope of making it the biggest and then becoming sad when it bursts. So humans are always empty as no materialistic object can ever fill their lust for 'more', but you were different sir; you never crave for more then; then why now?." Aiden didn't know what to reply so he chose silence, he didn't want them to know that someone else is residing in their master's body. He would try to solve the mystery on his own.

Aiden heard him out but wondered why he was being lectured on the topic. He realised that missing something does not depict any materialistic thing; rather it depicted something like.... He stopped as he could not describe it further. He stopped and agreed with the butler and said he would try to be happy and be satisfied with what he had, like he used to be. However, before that he needed to find out something. He ordered Vaahindi to book a ticket to Lihamantos. Vaahindi was surprised as why he needed to travel to such an underdeveloped area. Aiden replied that there was no particular reason; he just wants to use some of his money for the development of that area.

The butler told him that his chartered plane would be ready in two days and that he would inform the pilots. Aiden was shocked to see that Karan was so rich to have his own private plane. Yet, this did not make him happy. Aiden just nodded his head and told the butler not to disturb him as he was tired and needed some rest.

The butler went away and Aiden lay down. He looked out of the windows seeing unfamiliar sights and experiencing unfamiliar events. He did not have the slightest of the clues of what was going on but was sure that this was one of the plans of the Devil to punish him. According to the contract, Aiden's survival would lead to thousands of death through the curse so how come no one was dying from it. It could be that they are dying but without knowing why as according to the new deal with the Devil, people had forgotten all about the curse. Therefore, they were attributing deaths from curse to natural causes.

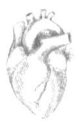

Chapter 4

OPPOSITE....

Two days passed by; the plane was now ready; Vaahindi had arranged Aiden's clothes and necessities and had loaded them on the plane. The plane was ready to take off. Aiden settled in his seat. He remembered that he could know people's past by just touching them. He tried touching himself to know about the body he was residing in, but to no avail; he still did not know how to use that power. He stopped trying and calmed down and waited patiently to reach his hometown.

The plane landed in Silaha, the nearest airport to Lihamantos as Lihamantos did not have any airport of its own. Aiden recalled that the last time he had directly travelled to and from Lihamantos by plane, but there was no time to think about these trivial matters now. As soon as they landed, there was a man with a placard with Karan's name written on it, he ignored him and walked out of the exit and hailed a taxi. As soon as he was about to step in the taxi, he remembered something and ran to the man with the 'Karan' placard. "Hello, I am Karan." The man smiled and said, "Good afternoon, Sir. I am Rafiq, your personal driver here in Silaha." Aiden smiled and told him to drive directly to Lihamantos. The driver suggested he must be tired after such a long journey so he should first have some food and rest at the hotel where a room has been booked for him. "Your ride to Lihamantos is scheduled at 8a.m tomorrow."

Rafiq questioned, "Would you like to go at the scheduled time or should we reschedule if you have any other plans?" Aiden realised he did not know anything about Karan's characteristics, his behaviour, his attitudes and was acting as Aiden all along giving the impression that he had gone crazy. He decided to learn about Karan and try to act like him. He tried to think how a rich person would act in such a situation. So he thought to stick to the schedule but then thought a 28-year person like Karan was most unlikely to work according to a schedule.

While thoughts revolved in his mind, the driver waited for him to reply. Minutes passed by and he was growing impatient so he could not wait any more and asked what Karan wanted to do. Aiden was not sure what to do and his thoughts were crushing him like a man between two trucks, so he decided to follow the schedule. He sat in the car and saw that the driver was talking to someone on the phone. Aiden realised that the driver is talking to Vaahindi; his butler. He realised that they are trying to figure out if he was Karan or not and were testing him and that the butler was being informed about the smallest details of his behaviour.

Aiden realised that from now on he had to take every step carefully and not rush anything. The car started for the hotel. Aiden kept imagining about his emotions and how he had faked his laughter in the police station thinking the inspector was the Devil. He had made a fool of himself everywhere and showed everyone he was mentally unstable.

They reached the hotel. Aiden was given his check-in card to the VIP lounge. He relaxed in his room, refreshed himself, had some food and rested. He came out with the serious look of a rich businessman. His voice deepened and he became stricter and tried to act less polite. The driver stopped the car after some time and asked if he could attend to an urgent phone call. Aiden nodded. Even after knowing that he was being watched and the driver mentioned everything to his butler he decided not to interfere.

The driver went out and talked to someone. He came after a while and started driving. Aiden asked him who he was talking to and he said it was someone from his home. Aiden just replied with an OK and they continued towards Lihamantos. Aiden wanted to meet his mother first so he told the driver to ask for the address of Evelyn Ermish's house. The driver asked everyone along the road and in the shops but no one had ever heard the name of Evelyn Ermish. The driver asked Aiden, "Sir, are you sure you want to find such a person?"

Aiden nodded. The driver asked if she was dead or alive. He looked at Aiden, his eyes twitching, and his Adam's apple constantly being up and down due to his gulping large amount of saliva. Aiden constantly looked at the driver as if his face was a spur to his imagination. The driver kept on calling him but it was as if he has gone into a deep and dreamy slumber with his eyes open.

The driver tried tapping him on the shoulder but his lean and feeble body that was erect slowly slumped. The driver was scared and rushed out of the front seat, opened the back door and placed a finger under Aiden's nose to check if he was still breathing. The whiff of air that hit his finger from Aiden's nostrils relieved him. He rushed the car to a nearby hospital. On the way, he felt someone tapping his shoulder and asking, "Have we reached yet?"

The driver looked behind and sighed, "Oh! You are all right! What happened to you, Sir, you seemed to have blacked out." Aiden explained it was rare neurological disorder he suffered from and that he was under medication and would soon be cured. The driver weaved a sigh of relief and said that no one could tell him about Evelyn Ermish. Aiden gave a confused look and accepted that Evelyn had never existed. He instructed the driver to drive back to the hotel.

There, Aiden told him to wait for some time. After an hour or two, he came out with a slip filled with the schedule for the next day. The driver went away. Aiden was silent. He was not imagining anything now. It seemed he was scared of his own thoughts, even if he was not feeling anything it was like he wanted himself to be scared of his own thoughts. He tried a diversion by watching TV or playing games on the PC. He was restless. He knew if he tried to sleep now, pre-sleep thoughts would crowd his mind reminding him of the dreadful scenes he had seen earlier. He realised that rest was not a good option. he kept on playing until he was completely exhausted and went into a deep and dreamless slumber on the chair itself. He woke up to a multitude of moving creatures. His pupils, moved from left to right vigorously remembering the scenes he did not want to see again. He realised he was in a dream that was being controlled by the thoughts in his subconscious. He had already planned a way out of those dreams.

He woke up, this time in the real world rather than in the dream world. It was 3 'o clock at night. He looked out of the window, thinking about the person's life in whose body he was in, realising that lack of imagination would make his life miserable and that he would be haunted for ever by his past and Karan's memories. He decided to work out a plan to know the whole life that Karan had been leading and how those dreams were related to him.

The schedule slip given to the driver was being checked by him when he suddenly saw that he had to find a man named Dr. Revman Muller. He went searching for the doctor as the list mentioned that he needed to find him within two days. He called some of his people and told them to search for a man named Revman Muller, a doctor.

The next day early in the morning the driver knocked on Aiden's room asking for a picture of that man, but Aiden's silence made it clear to him that except for the man's name, he had no other details. It was 6 in the morning and Aiden was all ready to follow the schedule he had prepared the day before. The first item on the list was to make a donation to an orphanage. He visited some of the nearby orphanages and donated millions. Next, he distributed food among beggars. He went to the demolished buildings and apartments and donated money for their restoration.

His next schedule was to visit the police station to find out about Dr. Revman. There, he was told to wait for the ACP. Just then, Aiden saw an apparition advancing towards him that came so close that he could feel the hot air gushing out of its nostrils. It was the ACP who asked him, "Do you think these kind acts and donations you are doing will save you from punishments and redeem your sins? Forty per cent of the Earth's human life was wiped out because of your silly revenge and mindless thought to create a better world. Their blood is on your hands and thus you can't escape that great a sin with such trivial donations. You need to go through the same hell as those lakhs of people have undergone due to your curse."

Aiden was speechless. He kept staring at the ACP. He felt someone was tugging him and soon that tugging turned into grabbing and pulling and it felt as if he was going from one frame to another. He fell into a dark pit and suddenly realised he had blacked out again but before he could fall deeper into the darkness he was pulled by a girl, a girl whose eyes were crystal clear, lips glossy, cheeks as clean and smooth as a piece of silk but the distinguished features did not give him a clear picture of her entire face. Before he could take a close look at her, he was conscious again.

He came to his senses and saw the driver and the ACP trying to wake him up. He looked around, tried to calm himself and then stood up and directly asked the ACP if he knew anything about a person named Dr. Revman. The ACP directed the inspector and the constables to search through the files for the man named Revman Muller and assured Aiden that they would inform him within a week. It was against the law to give information about anyone to outsiders but Aiden paid him a heavy bribe, which made the ACP agree to the illegal.

They left the place and the last item on the schedule was to visit a sea beach to spend some time alone with mother nature and sort out his thoughts. They went to a beach nearby. Aiden walked to the seashore and told his driver to come with him. He asked him very calmly with a smile on his face about what behavioural changes had he seen in him that he had mentioned to Vaahindi. The driver looked shocked. Aiden told him not to show any emotions as he himself was devoid of them since he had been reborn.

The driver realised that lying was not going to help so he spoke the truth, "Karan, whom Vaahindi knew from his childhood, is a strict but sensitive guy. He gets easily emotional over the smallest matters. Once he tried to file an FIR against a villain who treated a girl badly in a movie as part of his role. He cried like a child that day seeing the actress being treated so badly by the villain. Not only sadness but all other emotions were also heightened to the peak. The smallest of incidents would make him angry to a level of hurting others physically. The smallest of happiness or gifts would make him so grateful that he could sell his property for the giver. But you are the complete opposite. You are calm and composed without any emotions or expressions. It is as if Karan was cursed with 'excess' and you are cursed with 'nothingness' like the two sides of a coin; exact opposite. But both of you are same despite the fact that you claim to be someone named Aiden while the world recognises this face as Karan's. These are my observations about you that I mentioned to Vaahindi."

Chapter 5
DECAPITATED CHANCE

Aiden listened carefully and understood that every word he said was true. He was calm and composed in every situation as if he did not feel anything. He blanked out all of a sudden and the only characteristic that matched with Karan was his strictness. Karan did everything after preparing his schedule and following it strictly and that is what Aiden did. "So, you believe that I am not your master Karan?"

The driver was in a dilemma what to reply. "It's not about whether I believe or not. One man's trust won't make you Aiden because thousands would still agree that you are Karan. Appearances are deceptive but that's what the basis to believe anything in this world. If you look like Karan, no one will believe that you are Aiden. It's difficult for me and I am still in dilemma how you could be Aiden. Can you tell us where our Master Karan is?"

Aiden was not sure if being frank to him was a good idea or not but he realised that being trusted is much better than being crazy so he decided to do things on a hunch and tell him everything. "Your Master is right here. I am in his body and we are not playing some double role with the same body under different names." The driver further asked, "So you have possessed our Master's body?" "I don't know, maybe but I don't feel your

Master's presence here. It's possible that he is dead and the Devil put me here to continue his life so that Karan lives on."

The driver gave a questioning look and Aiden asked him if he had time to listen to his story. The driver laughed and said, "I am your slave, if you have the time to tell, then I have the time to listen." Aiden started narrating his story bit by bit without leaving out a single detail. He described how his parents had died when he was only five years old. He had been burned alive with his father but was given another chance by the Devil to live and avenge his parents' death. Seeing and realising the life history of his parents made him understand human life and the characteristics of a human that poisoned his mind in his childhood. This grew stronger after seeing his parents' death and with the help of the Devil he put a curse upon Earth that would begin working as soon as he took birth.

However, in the second life he was born into a normal family and that gave him ample experience about life and the realisation that some people lead normal and peaceful lives while others become violent and adventurous. In his previous life, his parents went through a difficult life. Gradually, he lost both his parents making him realise the pain of losing someone you love. He started working out the mystery of the deaths that he himself had started.

After remembering his past life, he felt miserable and realised how silly and futile the curse was including the idea to reform the world. He started working on how to end the curse, and heal those afflicted by it. while the curse had already killed many people, it used their life source to heal his own injuries. According to the Devil's contract, he could only be killed by someone he trusted and loved, or else he would be healed everytime he was injured, doesn't matter how serious the injury is. So, he concluded that he has to make his true friend go against him and kill him and thus he succeded. After reaching hell, the Devil said that his life energy and memories had to be wiped out completely as his existence in the timeline of the universe could revive the curse any time.

He finalised another deal that would make everyone forget that Aiden had ever existed and that there was never a curse rather it was a deadly virus outbreak, a pandemic. His mother and lover would be reborn and lead normal and peaceful lives.

After hearing all this, Karan's driver burst into laughter, but seeing the seriousness on his face he became silent. "You do narrate the best of stories, Sir." Aiden was confused. "I narrate?" "Oh sorry, you are not my sir, you are Aiden" the driver taunted him in a sarcastic tone. "The body you possess is of one of the greatest writers on this Earth. He is known as the master of mythic tales and as you are not Karan, you may not know it."

Saying this, he burst into laughter again. Aiden realised the mistake he had made by telling him the truth and swore never to work on his hunches again He cursed his fate and realised he is the unluckiest man ever alive. First he made a deal with untrustworthy devil, then he couldn't lead his life, now he had to lead someone's else's life and the only person he told the truth believes it to be a fairy tale because the person in whose body he relives is the greatest writer. He realised there is no use in thinking about all these, so he just decided to lead the life he is given. He told his driver to start the car. The driver's face lost all the laughter and a serious expression clouded his face, "You should read your own stories, may be trying to give the best stories to your readers has stressed you so much that you have made yourself a character of one of your books."

Aiden had nothing to say but just one last question to ask, "sometime ago you said that I and Karan are same, can you elaborate?" The driver looked at him and answered with a smile, "Both of you have curious minds and work on myths. You search for mythical people, meanwhile he searched for mythical places." Aiden realised it is futile to ask any more questions, so he just instructed him to head towards the hotel. After reaching there, he went directly to his room and locked it and refused any room service. He called Vaahindi and told him to prepare for his return in two days. He thought of going to sleep and not think about anything else.

Just then someone knocked. Aiden opened the door and saw his driver who started to talk about a tale. "Master, I think the character Aiden in your book spoilt his own chances of surviving with his loved ones." Aiden was confused and asked, "How?" In the previous life, Aiden had thought of all possibilities before reaching the conclusion of dying by the hands of his friends. As he was constantly imagining the other possibilities the driver started to talk again and Aiden saw that his legs and hands were trembling, eyes red and half closed, the driver couldn't even stand properly. He understood he was drunk thus told him to go away. He again locked the door without even seeing if the driver had gone away or was still standing there. He remembered that till now he doesn't even know his name. he decided to ask him the other day. He went to bed.

As he was about to sleep, he remembered the last words of the driver. "If you started the cure with a lower being, that is, the Devil then you should have stopped it with a higher being that is a God." Aiden realised that this could have been a possibility as being a regular human being he had met the Devil and made a deal with him. Thus there would have been a way to meet God who would have helped him get rid of the problem. He tried regretting but knew it was not an option.

He could not wait for two days to return home. His patience was wearing thin so he started looking for books online and was shocked to see that Karan had written 28 books, of which 17 were bestsellers. This was a good and profitable source of income. Karan had used the money to invest in stocks and when he had made enough, he established his own start-up and successfully reigned over other companies.

Aiden did not find anything else about his past or his personal life. He realised he could not rely on the internet to solve the riddles that life had played out in front of him. He decided to check out the books written by Karan to know his life story. A person's personal life and characteristics are reflected in his writings. He thought he would get some clues about Karan from his books, thus he decided to read his books once he reaches home.

He went to sleep but the dreadful scenes kept haunting him.

He stopped thinking about his past and imagining about Karan and fell into a deep slumber. He woke up the next morning, ate his fill, and went to discover more about Lihamantos. He went from place to place trying to look for where he used to live in and where his parents had their ancestral house. Aiden remembered Phobitos where his father was rumoured to have stayed when he left him at the age of five but Aiden realised, he should not rush from one point to another. He needed to know all about Karan to proceed to the next step. He saw how poorly developed the city of Lihamantos was. There is no railway station or airport in the area. He remembered how he had lived in Lihamantos when it was developing, with railway stations and airports already present it wasd developing in medical and education sectors, rather than that the transportation sectors were already developd, but here in new Lihamantos every thing is a dream for the people as it is so underdeveloped that people had to make a queue even to get water two times a day.

For now Aiden banished these thoughts from his mind. He decided to enjoy his homeland or what he thought to be his homeland for twenty five years. He discovered places he had visited in his previous lives and realised how different they were. He is in 2023 in Lihamantos which meant it should have been the same, but why did it look so different and not in a good way. These thoughts crowded his mind so much that he could not even nap properly.

He tried many a time not to think about anything and just concentrate on having fun in his homeland but to no avail. The questions came rushing in. He went to a nearby stall and was drinking tea when he saw the news on TV about the death of a rich businessman by heart attack. His eyes widened upon seeing this news, not because that someone died due to heart attack, but because of the fact that the one who died was none other than Jacob. He recognised his friend from his previous life. He started wondering that his friends might be leading a happy life and him being born again had killed him as the curse has been reactivated. Or possibly, the curse had already begun affecting people and that he came to know of it now only as he had not watched the news since, he had been reborn, he realised that Lihamantos must be in such condition due to him being born again and most of its population got wiped out thus leaving the city underdeveloped..

Just then his phone rang interrupting his thoughts. Vaahindi called to let him know about the death of his friend, Jacob, the rich businessman whose death he just saw on the news. He said that he had been invited to Jacob's funeral. Aiaden tried to be a little happy that even in this life he is still Jacob's friend but then he remembered that it was not him that got invited, rather it was Karan. The police were investigating his death to know if it was due to natural cause or a planned murder. Aiden hung up the phone, being sure of the fact that he had been reborn into the true world and it was not the hell so, he rushed to the police station to ask if they had found anything about Revman and Evelyn Ermish. The ACP said nothing had been found yet and hearing this Aiden returned. He sat on the pavement wondering how the curse was still haunting the world, why he is still alive and the greatest question that currently struck his mind is how does Jacon know Karan?

Aiden now realised that that on the day he had died and his existence was wiped out, the Devil might have made some mistake. Therefore, the curse had not stopped and had wiped out most of the people. Only some were surviving to repopulate the Earth. Realising it was a pandemic, people stopped thinking about it and got habituated to it. The Devil had made sure he was born again in a new world created by the curse, the reformed world. Every time a new possibility like this struck him a new reason arose making the possibility a mistake. However, this time he saw no reason to find fault in this possibility.

He realised that it was the same world but the curse was still in effect and so needed to be wiped out before it afflicted another phase of human beings. This possibility needed some proof. He decided to unearth some. One thought that haunted him is that he has no close friends on this Earth so even if he proves that the curse is still in effect them there is now way he could stop it, So he decided to take one step at a time. First to prove that the curse still existed and second to cure it, like he did in his previous life with his friends. The only difference in this life was he did not care about people dying or he tried to care but couldn't. He decided he would wait for the funeral where he hoped to find some proof to this mystery.

Till then he would try to find out more about Karan to know why he had been transferred into someone else's body with whom he did not have any connection. His mobile vibrated with a notification. He saw a profit in the 12th market stock of 120 crore. He realised now he has to manage all these things. He sat down to do trading, but did not know much about it. He called his driver and assistants and told them that he would be testing them. "Anyone who can earn me a profit of 150 crore in the 12th market will be rewarded."

His assistants were stock specialists. Karan who loved trading had hired them for continuous help and assistance. Aiden sighed a breath of relief, he would watch them dong trading so as to gain some knowledge and experience about it. He now knew that this life would be much harder than the previous one as now he had to live someone else life—be an author, a businessman—and search for the life story of someone whom he barely knows and solve the mystery of the curse. He realised how painful this life would be and remembered that at least he had his friends in his previous life to help him out, but here he has to work alone to achieve all these. He remembered that he has one positive point in all these that is he would not be feeling pain or sorrow this time even if he wanted to.

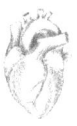

Chapter 6
STARTS AGAIN

The quest for a solution started again. The plane was ready to take off but at the last moment there were some technical issues. Aiden was getting ready to leave for Silaha but as soon as he got the message that the plane would be delayed by eight hours he went back into his room. He had no enthusiasm to solve the mystery and neither frustration due to obstruction in his works. It was as if he had lost all interest in life. He knew he was not his old self anymore. He needed to solve his problems as soon as possible. Thinking so much about these matters tired him and he fell asleep.

After an hour or two he woke up and called room service to order a large quantity of food. It would have been enough for a person to feed on for two days but Aiden was so hungry that he polished all up by himself. He had watched TV for half an hour when his driver knocked and told him they were ready to leave for Silaha. Aiden left the room while his assistants carried his luggage. They drove to the airport in Silaha. They reached there in three hours and Aiden left for Milatintia where Karan lived. He is now more or less acquainted to Karan's lifestyle and his attitude, by talking to his driver on the sea shore that day. Even if he could not have emotions, he was trying his best to fake them.

Though people now started believing that his insanity is gone but, his assistants and drivers were confused why their Master was acting so strangely, showing new characteristics everyday, they were really confused if he was truly their master or not. After reaching Milatintia, Aiden tried to act like Karan even with his butler. He tried to cry seeing sad movies but could not as tears are a part of sadness and he was unable to shed them, even after faking expression of sadness he couldn't bring out tears. He tried to hurt himself so that the pain brought tears to his eyes, but it was all in vain, he felt the pain but he has become so shallow that nothing could bring out a pint of emotion in him. Finding his butler not able to believe him, he went on increasing hurting himself physically, but all in vain.

Vaahindi told him to stop and just act naturally in any way he felt. No one would call him crazy until he acts as a character in his own imaginary stories. Aiden understood that the driver had told him everything. He agreed to do as the butler advised as he was also tired of acting.

The butler told him they would go to Jacob's funeral the next day and to his death ceremony the day after it. He requested Karan to act normally and not try anything weird at the ceremony that would make people suspect him. Besides, the police would also be there to pay their respects and also see if anything could help in their investigation as they still suspect that this could be case of murder. Aiden agreed and asked the butler where he could find the books that he had written.

The butler looked at him strangely and then pointed towards the top shelf of the cupboard in a corner of the room. After Vaahindi went away, Aiden locked the room from inside, opened the cupboard, and saw all the 28 books there. Every book had it's three version in there, the handwritten one, the typed one and the published one. Karan used to write the stories by hand rather than typing them and keep the handwritten copies even after they were typed and edited. After the story was printed, he would add a copy to his collection. He was highly obsessed with his stories and books. This was evident by seeing how clean and organised the shelf was.

Aiden decided to read the books to find out about Karan's life. All the books were fiction but many authors do put some incidents from their life and add some fantasy to it to make it enjoyable, Aiden decided to piece out the incidents which can truly occur in a human life and put them together to complete the puzzle. He started from book-1, all the books were properly organised and kept according to the year it got published. All the books were numbered from 1 to 28 and kept serially. Book-1 was titled "King of Dreeks". Aiden read the summary and it truly gave him the vibe of a bestseller. He realised he won't get bored thus started right away.

After five hours of reading a 250-page book, Aiden realised that it was of no use as it was pure fiction and nothing could be linked to real life. From the novel, Aiden came to know that Dreek in the title was the name of a place, a place where till date people believe in mythological gods and powers. They appoint the king from the royal lineage but they are highly developed and is the richest place on Earth. No outsider is allowed into the city and no insider ever comes out. Since 1786, the Dreeknians had lost faith in humans from outside their city and they cut off all connections with them after declaring themselves independent and out of the world. Many tried to go to Dreek and learn about its culture but none of them had returned and those who returned had lost their sanity. The lone person who had returned safe and sound would not speak anything about it.

Aiden rushed downstairs to ask Vaahindi about that place. The butler related all that his Master had told him. "In 1786, the people of Dreek were betrayed by their king due to the interference of an outsider. The king's rule became inefficient and so they had to kill him and shut their city to outsiders. Anyone whose ancestry was not Dreeknian was killed. Other countries tried to wage war against Dreek but their weapons failed to defeat them.

The countries came to the conclusion that the Dreeknians had one of the world's most developed weapons and their science and technology was far more developed than their own, so it was futile to wage any war against them or try to take over that place. However, they wondered how the Dreeknians had achieved such advancement and what had happened to their king , how they developed such mercenaries and how the king had betrayed his countrymen but all these remained a mystery. Only recently, a person had returned from Dreek but he had not spoken since.

Only yesterday, he started talking but was highly scared to say anything about the Dreeknians and their city. "Can I meet him?" Aiden asked. the butler refused and said that anyone who ever put their foot in Dreek and returned was jailed in the 'Zebrocca' prison. The prisoners are used as subjects for investigation and experimentation. The results and the prisoners who have been experimented on are kept confidential. No one can meet them except for appointed government officials.

Aiden went into his room realising that the book he thought to be a fiction may not be a pure fiction and wondered that Karan might be a Dreeknian as he had written most of his stories set in the city of Dreek. However, there was no reference of the king's betrayal in Karan's story. He realised that the setting was only to make people curious and ensure the sales of the books. It was neither the truth nor were all the stories related to Dreeks. He stayed up all night researching about Dreek on internet and also read some of the books written by Karan. It was 4 o'clock in the morning.

Aiden was reading the fifth book when he started feeling drowsy and fell asleep. After three hours, the butler came to wake up his

(AD 48)

Master to get ready for work. Seeing the room in a mess and his Master fast asleep on the study table he understood that he had slept late. He did not disturb him and called the assistants to carry him to his bed and cover him up with a sheet. The butler looked at the research his master had done in the night and thought that this time his Master may not have been weird but actually telling the truth. Thinking this, he went away.

Aiden woke up at 11 a.m. and rang the bell. Vaahindi came running. Aiden told him to prepare his breakfast. He freshened up, went to the dining hall, and had his breakfast. He looked downcast and moved his hands through his hair in a tensed manner. He asked Vaahindi, "Why are you answering all my questions, taking care of me rather than taking me to a psychiatrist or asking about the crazy things I am saying?" Vaahindi smiled and replied, "It's not new for us Master. When you are to write a new story, you act as the protagonist and see those around as the other characters of that story. You would also assign us the characters we are to play, but this time we started to doubt at the beginning when you went to the girl you had promised not to see even on her deathbed, and you kept on acting without assigning us any roles. Your weird actions of not remembering who you were and calling yourself by another name made us think that you are trying something new and serious for another unique story. So, we stopped reacting to your changes.

However, seeing your

research paper last night made me doubt you a little as Master had already researched a lot on that city before writing about it in the stories." Aiden looked at him sharply, and then turned his head around to look at the portraits of Karan hanging on the walls. He wanted to ask the butler more about Karan's family, his parents and more about his love life and why Karan had sworn never to meet Sihira again but he felt kind of embarrassed to ask these questions as from the time of his rebirth in Karan's body, he had been acting weird for these people.

The question he asked leaving all doubts behind was whether Karan had met with an accident on 22 June. The butler replied in the affirmative and Aiden understood that, that was the day he died and on the same day only Karan also met an accident so it was the day on which Karan had been replaced by him in Karan's body. The butler said a truck had hit Karan's car but luckily, he was safe and escaped even with major injuries. The most astonishing thing was there was not a single wound nor a scar on his body as if the accident had never happened.

Some locals who were passing by said the truck driver had intentionally hit Karan's car and dashed away after talking to someone on the phone. Aiden asked if the driver had been caught and Vaahindi said two persons were caught two days earlier but due to his Karan's weird behaviour he had not mentioned him of it. Aiden knew where to start looking for the origin of Karan but just as he was about to leave, Vaahindi gave him a letter that was marked 'confidential'. It was from Jacob's father. A short paper sticking on the note said, "This is a confidential note written by Jacob before his death, and was meant to be read only by you so we are sending it without reading it. We have not told the police about it. If the letter says anything related to our son's death, do help us."

Aiden took out the note from the envelope. It only had three words and Aiden knew they were written hastily. He realised something was fishy and he had to find the answer. He told Vaahindi to get his car ready and that he was leaving for Jacob's house immediately. The butler was confused why his Master was in such a hurry. Just then, he noticed the folded note that has fallen from his master's hand.

Vaahindi picked it up. His eyes opened wide, hands trembled, his breathing became heavy, and his lips muttered the words, "I was killed."

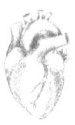

Chapter 7
DON'T RETURN TO...

Aiden reached Jacob's house, an it was a total sad and pathetic surrounding, he saw his parents crying. Seeing him, both of them ran and hugged him. Aiden tried to console them and tried to tell Rivet Avera, Jacob's father about the note but as soon as he began, Rivet pinched him on the palm indicating him to keep quiet about the note as they were being watched. Aiden wanted to cry, but as usual he couldn't. Thus he just acted with a sad expression. He consoled them saying, "Don't cry, Jacob will always be alive in our hearts." He paused to stress on that sentence.

Hearing this, Jacob's parents tried to express their happiness but Aiden hugged them tightly burying their faces against his chest so that no one is able to see the expression change on their face. He told them, "I will look after the rituals and rites, don't worry. I know as a parent you can't face up to the death of your own son." Both the parents kept listening to Aiden. Aiden told them that he had to go and make the arrangements.

As he was about to leave, Jacob's parents called out to him several times but Aiden just walked towards his car. After some time, he realised that they were calling out the name 'Karan'; the body in which he is residing. After realisation he turned around and looked at them. He gestured that he would handle everything and left. Aiden drove home.

On the way back to Karan's house, he felt as if everyone on the road was staring at him. Even those in the shops did so. Feeling uncomfortable he sped home. He tried to get the note he had received but he couldn't find it, realising he may have left the note at home and how it could be dangerous for Jacob, he called Vaahindi and asked him if he had seen any paper on his table.

Vaahindi gave him the note without a word and went into the kitchen to prepare lunch. Aiden opened the note and read it again. He looked sternly at the butler. Aiden ran upstairs to his room. He fell on the bed and tried to sleep but his mind was churning with all sorts of thoughts that kept him awake. His hands shook. He tried to sit up but his body was uncontrollable. His eyes opened slowly.

His heart stopped beating. His inner self came out of his body and passed through every object, the bed, the floor, the ground. He fell eventually on firm ground with such a bang that everyone started looking towards him. This 'everyone' didn't referred to humans rather it referred to the demons staring down at him. He realised he is in hell, at last after so much hard work and living a hellish life finally he gets to meet the one because of whom he had to suffer. He tried calling out 'Lucifer' . Just then, a demon dressed like Lucifer told him that Lucifer was no more in hell as he had become a god and was ruling the heavenly and earthly realms.

The Demon dressed like Lucifer was none other than Satan who told "But he didn't go to heaven to rule, rather he keeps suffering in prism so as to redeem for his sins; and its all because of you.". Aiden remembered Karan's driver's words, "If a lowly being started the curse, a higher being can cancel it." Realising that Lucifer could help him now but seeing the wrath and hatred in Satan's eyes he saw no way of meeting Lucifer. Satan warned him that if he returned there again, he, the king of hell, Lucifer's son, would give him the most painful life on Earth.

He could have given him a painful death right at that moment but he didn't want to defy his father's wishes;Lucifer, who wanted to give Aiden another chance to live his life like a normal human, so Satan had to obey his father. "I would have taken out your heart and played handball with it in front of you." Saying this, he kept staring at Aiden with the same angry look while the other demons started laughing. Aiden was confused and asked what he was talking about. Before Satan could reply, Aiden heard the sound of knocking and suddenly he felt as if he was being pulled upwards. In the blink of an eye, he was back on Earth in Karan's room.

Hearing shouting for Karan and persistent knocking on the door, Aiden opened it and saw Vaahindi and the other workers standing outside. Vaahindi was tensed and asked if he was all right. Aiden told him everything was fine. Vaahindi gave a sigh of relief and turned to leave but just then Aiden tapped on his shoulder and asked, "Why have you come to my room?"

Vaahindi said that he had been worried as his Master had not been responding. "What was the need to call me in the first place?" The butler said he wanted to ask if he would like his turkey spicy or with a pinch of sugar.

"How did I usually like?" Aiden asked questioningly. Vaahindi said, mostly spicy; in fact, you love everything spicy." Aiden looked at him, smiled, and replied "Then what was the meaning of asking?". Vaahindi understood the tone and went away.

Aiden locked the door. He searched for the name, Reinese in his contacts, but couldn't find it. He thought that if the same Jacob who he was friends with was also Karan's friend then Karan must also be having a friend named Reinese. He rushed down to ask Vaahindi if he knew anyone named Reinese Stitterman who was supposed to be Karan's friend. Vaahindi replied that he happens to know a Stitterman who is a famous scientist in the Ziranso lab but it isn't Reinese, it's Joey Stitterman.

Aiden asked if he was friend with Joey. Vahindi shook his head. Aiden nodded and walked out of there and drove to the hospital where Sihira was admitted. He went to her ward and saw she was eating some fruits. Seeing Karan, tears rolled down her cheeks. Aiden, acting as Karan, hugged her. She sobbed while hugging him.

Aiden stroked her hair gently and told her not to be sad. He told her that something weird has happened to him and that he was incapable of displaying any emotions and feelings thus he needed her help. Aiden told her that he could not trust anyone except her as she was the only one who loved him unconditionally, Aiden took a shot at it, that she may be the true love of Karan.

Sihira looked at him and asked what help he wanted. He drew the curtains and locked the door and then took up the doctor's pad and pen and told Sihira they would not speak but write their conversation and speak by gestures. Aiden wrote his questions on the paper and Sihira answered them likewise.

A: Do you know any local doctors or bio-scientists?

S: Yes, some.

A: Do they work for any agency?

S: I don't know much, they are either my father's friends or relatives.

A: Is there anyone your father do not know?

S: Let me check my phone, I can't recall clearly.

Aiden gave her, her phone placed on the table near him. She unlocked it and started scrolling down her contacts. After five minutes or so, she pointed to a number on her screen. Aiden noted it down and started writing again.

A: Is she a good one?

S: Yes, she has a small but her own bio-research laboratory.

A: A friend of yours and no contact with your father?

S: A very good friend of mine, but I haven't contacted her since months; she doesn't like my father; in fact she hates him.

Aiden got the perfect person for what he had in mind. He bid farewell to Sihira and told her he might not be able to meet her ever again but if he stayed alive, he would take her with him. She became tensed upon hearing this and Aiden realised that he might not be able to leave as she may cling to him and not let him leave, so he laughed and told her that he was joking. Sihira sighed and hugged him, he patted her on the shoulder and went away.

Walking out of the hospital, he felt he was being watched but pretended he did not know about it.

Aiden drove to the nearest ISD booth and called the number he had obtained from Sihira. A girl answered, "Remiri here." Aiden told her that he is Karan and he got her number from Sihira. Remiri in an angry tone replied "Ohh! Now the queen remembers me when she needs my help. Where was she when I tried to reach her, when I was in problem, she didn't call me once." She was about to hang up the call when Aiden told her how Sihira met with a severe accident and also lied to her that she has been house arrested before her accident thus she couldn't contact her. Remiri somewhat convinced by his talks asked him the cause for calling her. Aiden told her that he needed her help. He told her they couldn't meet openly as it would be a threat to both their lives. He asked her if she could test blood on the micromolecular level to check for some neurotoxins in it.

Remiri replied it was not possible in her clinic as they did not have the advanced tools needed for the purpose. She could send the blood for testing at the Ziranso Lab under an anonymous name to keep the identity of the sender hidden, but it would cost a lot. Before she could say anything else, Aiden interrupted her and offered to pay her double the charges as soon as she gave him the results.

Remiri upon hearing the amount of money she was being offered she immediately agreed. Aiden hung up the call and returned to his house and drew some of his blood with a syringe from the first aid box. He hid it in his pocket and went to the supermarket. At the chips section, he slid the mini bottle containing the blood behind one of the chips packets.

Remiri who was already there knew Karan as earlier she had seen him a few times with Sihira; saw him doing it and as soon as he left after buying some items, she walked towards the chips section and found the bottle containing blood. She collected the blood sample. Slid it into her pocket and left. She went to her clinic and told her assistant to take the blood sample to Ziranso for performing micromolecular tests to check the presence of toxins.

Her assistant submitted the sample to Ziranso Lab and informed Remiri that the result would be available after 3-4 days. Aiden had breakfast, lunch and dinner outside rather than at Karan's house. Even after knowing that he was constantly being watched, he behaved normally. As he was laying in a hotel room when suddenly he remembered he had to do something. He rushed home.

He asked Vaahindi about the two truck drivers who had been caught and jailed. Vaahindi told him they were arrested and were in jail. Aiden told him he was going to meet them. Vaahindi tried to stop him by referring to them as dangerous criminals but Aiden looked at him doubtfully and said that he need not worry as he would be under police protection.

Aiden went to the police station but they turned down his request to meet the culprits saying it was against the law. Aiden murmured, "I knew it." He called his lawyer who showed the inspector the victim's rights; to meet the culprit who hurt the victim or tried to hurt him. The inspector then told the constable to take Aiden to cell 12 C. Aiden went in to talk while the inspector stood outside.

Aiden asked the drivers who had sent them to kill him. The drivers fell to their knees and pleaded to be released saying it was only an accident and they had no intention to kill Karan. Meanwhile Aiden was about to talk to them and tell them he will try to release them by taking back the case, the drivers gestured him to tell them his address. Aiden understood the task, and bent down to pick them up as they were kneeling down. In this process while he bent down his face was not visible in the camera and during this he whispered his address to the drivers. The drivers just nodded and then the three of them stood. Aiden patted them on their shoulders and walked out of the cell, signed the bail papers for them. He mentioned it was an accident and the drivers had no bad intention. They were released and Aiden returned home.

Vaahindi came to know what his Master had done and scolded him. "This was the reason I was not letting you meet them. You are a soft-hearted person who melts at the simplest of sadness. You have released your own murderers. Once they missed the chance but this time they will make sure to kill you." Aiden told him to calm down as nothing would happen to him.

After consoling him he went to his room. The two drivers rushed to their boss; sitting on a chair in a garage with a black hoodie, the person gave out a wicked smile on getting Karan's. He packed a parcel and couriered it to Karan's address. Meanwahile Aiden was impatient for his blood test results. For the last two days, he had been working on his stocks and they had shown a steady profit for Karan's company.

Aiden frequently called Remiri inquiring about the blood report; every time he was that told it had not come. The next day, there was a parcel for Karan. Aiden ran downstairs, grabbed it, and ran to his room. He ordered Vaahindi not to disturb him for the next two hours.

Aiden opened the parcel and read his blood test reports. He saw the presence of neurotoxins. He wanted to know more about it so he hid the report and rushed to the nearby ISD booth to contact Remiri.

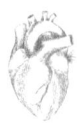

Chapter 8

BLOOD VERSUS POISON

Aiden asked Remiri if she had checked his report or not and she replied that the results were shocking. She described what she had found in the result. "You have been fed these toxins from a long time. They are a kind of neurotoxins that once it enters the human body through food, they run into the blood stream and as our blood tries to remove any unwanted substance it does the same with the toxins but instead of being destroyed it breaks and starts multiplying. The toxins do not loose its potentiality and breaking, it maintains it's poisonous effects. The poison content in each micro molecule doesn't lessen after breaking up, one of its micro molecule is as poisonous as when it was a part of the macromolecule, that flows along with the blood and accumulates near the aorta region in the heart that in result lessens the amount of blood flow into and out of the heart thus choking it stopping the heart resulting in death , and all this takes a maximum of four to five days. Repeated blood flow washes off those accumulated toxins, and in a short period of time after death that is within three to four hours the toxins will dissolve in the blood without leaving behind a trace of it's presence, and normal blood tests even on micromolecular level won't be able to detect it until and unless the company or institution has machineries like Ziranso lab; As for the sample you had sent for testing, they found the presence of those neurotoxins but the particles had already broken up into micro molecules and was on the verge of dissolving, which means whoever blood you sent, that man or woman is already dead but you may have collected the blood sample within some hours that's why we could detect the toxins. But how did you collect a dead man's blood sample, that too just after his death?"

Aiden absent-mindedly told her that it was his blood sample. Remiri was shocked knowing those neurotoxins are highly efficient and can surely kill any human, and even a small dose was enough to kill an elephant within a week. "yet you are still alive, and no new particles of those substance had been found in your blood which means those toxins are no more being fed to you." She wanted to know how he has survived. Aiden didn't give much heed to her questions and with a grave tone told her not to tell anyone about this. Saying this he hung up the phone not letting her ask any further questions. He put the folded report in his pocket and walked out of the house.

He did not feel any anger towards anyone, even if this was the peak of angry period in any human's life. Among everything; eye gouging, pinching, cutting organs, betrayal is the most hurtful thing anyone can do, and here he was standing; betrayed by his own people but still feeling nothing . He was missing his emotions. His expressions were still calm and composed. He went to a nearby park, devoid of any people. As soon as he reached there he started shouting and hitting hard objects, but to no avail; no frustration, no anger, no sadness, the nly thing he felt was the immense pain in his legs and hands that he got by hitting objects.

After a brief walk in the park he returned home. He called Vaahindi to his room. Vaahindi followed him. Aiden told him to bring him some food and in a taunting voice added "without sugar and without poison." Vaahindi was shocked but before Aiden could speak further, Vaahindi told him "It was my duty to do so". Aiden was shocked to hear this as according to him, the people whom the servants serve, their duty is to protect their master and not to kill him, but the first question he asked was "If you could have killed me with the neurotoxins then why did you try to kill me in an accident?"

Vaahindi said, "First we tried to kill you by accident and if that fails we were given the neurotoxin to inject it into the body of the target."

"Why don't you use the toxins at the beginning?"

Vaahindi said those toxins cost millions of rupees so they try to do without it, if possible

"Who is it who wants to kill me?"

Vaahindi answered that no one was allowed to name him but "I betrayed you even after I worked for you for more than fifty years, and I also failed the duty given to me, so now it is my duty to serve you properly, thus I will tell you about your killer." Aiden was struck by what he had said, in the whole sentence said by Vaahindi the only thing that caught his attention was 'I worked for you for more than fifty years'. "I am 28 years old so how could you have worked for me for 52 years?" Hearing this question Vaahindi got a little shocked. He exclaimed, "So you are truly not our Master 'Karan', you are someone else. Even after rebirth, Karan never forgot his past life."

Aiden asked, "Rebirth?"

Vaahindi pulled the curtains together, locked the door and played a movie on the TV at high volume. These all precautions were taken by him so that no one would be able to see or hear them. He sat down with Aiden to tell him all about Karan. He told him that every 70 years Karan died and was reborn remembering his past. Being so sensitive, he would remember the people he had lost and break into tears. Most of his time would pass in sadness as he had seen many of his loved ones die while he lived but the curse never him forget them, "but I had started doubting you from the day you became conscious again; as rebirth starts with our master being born again but this time you woke up after losing consciousness and the fact that someone else is in his body shows that our master is dead but his body has been possessed by someone else."

He said that it was some kind of a curse, that Karan has to face; so much of emotions and to take rebirth and live forever while his near and dear ones keep dying. With this he said that this is all he knows about his master. The butler admitted that the neurotoxins and the accident were all done to show the killer that you are dead, but the killer doesn't know that you reborn with your memories intact. Aiden stared at the butler thinking, "So I started the curse in my previous life for other people and this life the whole life is cursed for me, but wait; I can make the most of it. If I die, then Karan's self may take over this body in rebirth so I have to survive. I can lead a normal human life that was taken away from me by the Devil." but with this life he has lost the essence of humanity, the most important thing that makes humans human; 'emotions.' He needed to get back his emotions. He kept all this a secret from Vaahindi.

Aiden asked Vaahindi "Can Karan be killed before the age of seventy?" Vaahindi nodded and said that his master can be killed by any disease or anyone can kill him anytime before the age of seventy, and if any calamity doesn't strike his life then he dies automatically at the age of seventy, not a day before or after that.

Aiden continued his questions; what happens to the body after Karan dies. Vaahindi told him that he burns his body, the body miraculously burns along with the bones all dissolving into thin air and even if he doesn't burn it, in three to four days the body automatically turns into dust leaving behind no trace. Karan then takes birth at some new place to some new parents and grows up to look exactly the same, it is as if the body returns to it's soul. Aiden asked him "Then how did he replace Karan in his body, if after dying his body tries to return to it's soul then how come the body allowed another soul to reside in it?" The butler replied doubtfully "May be because when we found him, his heart was missing, so it may be possible that his soul was in his heart and he was taken along with it. Everytime my master died his physical body would start to turn into dust so that he can take birth again but this time it didn't happen, so we took a shot by planting an artificial heart into the body and it worked but the adverse effect was instead of our master someone else woke up in his body." Even if the butler was unsure of that theory Aiden was sure that as soon as another heart was implanted, the Devil put him in that body. However, the only question that remained unanswered was 'why were the emotions missing?' He needed to know the answers.

He did not know which death would be his last one and the body would again be taken up by it's true master, so he needed to work in a manner that he did not face death anymore and solve the mystery while he is alive. Just then, someone rang the bell. Vaahindi took permission and left to find out. It was another parcel for Karan. Vaahindi, without checking the contents because he was feeling guilty about the betrayal, took the parcel directly to his Master's room. Even if he new the person sitting in Karan's room is not his master but he still tried to serve him so that no one doubts them.

Aiden did not want to show he did not have feelings, so he showed that he was angry by changing his expressions strangely. Vaahindi knocked on the door. Aiden told him to enter in and place the parcel on the table. Meanwhile, the Ziranso research centre contacted Remiri, Remiri thinking that they might have contacted her to ask if she had got the reports or not, so before they could speak she told them that she had received the reports; she was about to hang up the call when the person told her that he and his team wanted to know about the person whose blood sample was sent to them for testing.

She lied to them that she did not know who he she received the call from an unknown number, and when she checked it, it was from an ISD booth. So it is hard to capture him. She had an idea so she told them that if they promised to pay her handsomely and also keep her name on the list of scientists who found a cure for cancer , would give them the person's name and address within two days. Ziranso has been working to find the cure for cancer since three years and they have almost found it and are waiting for the government approval to release it. Remiri wanted to earn name and fame thus she wanted to be among those who found the cure for the most deadliest disease. The researchers agreed to her demand.

After they hung up, the researchers laughed to their heart's content. "That silly girl thought we were only going to find a cure for cancer," said one of them. "She can't see the much higher goals we are aiming for." These people will always be fools," said another researcher.

Remiri went to the hospital to meet Sihira and talk to her about her health. Seeing Remiri Sihira showed her anger that Remiri didn't even pay her a visit. Remiri also wanted to fireback by saying that she also didn't come to her rescue during her hard times but she chose to remain silent as she had work to be done and only Sihira could help her. She apologised to her and asked her if she is all right or not. After some girly talks Remiri asked her is she could get the name and address of the person whom Sihira gave her number to. At first Sihira hesitated but Remiri showed her the report and lied to her that the man's blood is poisoned by a lethal neautoxin and that toxin is killing that man, and that it is a slow poison for him. Therefore, she needed to find him and treat him as soon as possible as by now his blood might surely have affected many of his internal organs.

Sihira could not understand what to do, so to protect Karan she gave her his contact number. As soon as Remiri got it, she bid farewell to Sihira and wished her to get well soon and went away. Sihira realised that something is not right so she followed her silently. Sihira hid behind a pillar and As Remiri reached outside she called someone and said "I got the contact number. As soon as you send me the payment, I will give it to you."

Sihira realised that she had been betrayed. Still not being properly healed she couldn't follow her or didn't had the strength to stop her so she returned to her ward and called Karan and told him that Remiri is planning to sell him to some research lab because of his rare blood or something. She couldn't tell properly as she couldn't hear clearly but is sure that Remiri ratted him out for some money. Aiden asked how she knew about it and Sihira told him the whole story but added that she had given Remiri a random number rather than his.

Aiden thanked her and hung up, he realised that problems are now pouring down on him like rain during cyclone, so he has to work fast. He opened the parcel he just received to find a box in it. He tried to open it but could not, he didn't have patience so he just kept it on the night stand and started planning how to escape the people and the police if the lab exposed the blood sample, because he knew that many bigshots are behind the working of the lab.

It was late at night, and the silence had fed on the sound and had spread everywhere. While Aiden was busy in his thoughts, in the silence of the night he heard a sound. It was the sound of a beating heart and it was not his. He closed his eyes and tried to focus on its direction and deduced that it was from inside the box. He looked carefully at it and saw a small hole in one of its corners. Aiden put in one of his fingers and realised it was a fingerprint scanner, a red light reflected off his finger before turning green. The box opened like a Chinese magic box.

Aiden couldn't think for some moment as if he was dumbstruck to see something unexpected, it was really unexpected. The sight left even the emotionless Aiden shocked. He was about to fall into a dark pit again when suddenly he came to his senses and stared at the open box that revealed a beating heart and a note by its side. "Of Karan, to Karan." Now Aiden knew why the two drivers had taken his address. Aiden contacted the number that was on the slip, present inside the box. The person at the other end began speaking as soon as he picked up, "I don't have much time to listen to your questions so I would just jump to the point. We were the ones who were given the contract to kill you but we couldn't. So we acted that accident and took away your heart so that no one can kill you.

The heart kept on beating even after being removed and I am one of the Dreeknians and know their legend. So, in the name of Dreek I return you your heart, but I can't tell you the name of the person who gave me your contract, but you will get your answers once you find Jacob and Reinese, my only wish is to see my birthplace safe and secure. Please return the happiness to it. Contact Remiri through Sihira."

Saying this, the man hung up. He and the two drivers prepared to leave the place, but before they could do so, they were shot dead by snipers, who have been aiming at them from top of a building for some three to four minutes. Aiden realised that in his haste he had called from his own phone which meant his enemy would have listened to their conversation, as phone tapping and tracking is not a myth in the new age. He tried calling the same number again, to learn more about him, but it was picked up by another man. He warned Aiden that he should hide or it would be too late and that the next call would be his last.

Aiden laughed and said, "Do bring your missiles; guns are not enough to kill me." Saying this he hung up, grabbed his coat and the box containing Karan's heart, and rushed to the hospital, on his way he realised that the box can be transformed into a card with the contents still present in it. He was shocked by the technology and wondered who are these Dreeknians who had such advanced technologies. He reached the hospital and saw three men going into Sihira's ward. He went to the door and eavesdropped on their conversation. They were asking her for Karan's location but Sihira refused and said that she is the love of his life and if they hurt her Karan will hunt them down and dig them in ground. They began forcing her. Aiden could wait no longer as they may hurt her so he broke in, took the doctor's knife, and stabbed it in one of the men's eyes. Another of the men tried to catch him but he pushed him and he hit his head against a steel desk. The third one was a tough one, but Karan's body was strong enough to block all his attacks; Aiden punched him on the nose, and as he shrieked and fell down with excruciating pain Aiden removed his hands from his face and kept punching him.

The man writhed in pain and didn't have the power to stand. Aiden removed the saline needles from Sihira's body and carried her in his arms and went upto the car. With the help of Sihira Aiden drove to Remiri's clinic. Reaching there, Aiden and Sihira searched for Remiri but suddenly heard a sound from inside another room. They slowly walked to the door and opened it to find an injured Remiri hiding there.

She hugged Sihira and exclaimed how happy she was to see them. Sihira pushed her away and looked at her disgustingly. Remiri realised that her betrayal has been caught and thus apologised that she should not have betrayed her but now they needed to save her. Sihira refused but then Remiri said something that caught Aiden's attention. She promised she would tell them Jacob's whereabouts. Sihira angrily shouted at Aiden not to help her but Aiden told her that it is the need of the hour and he needs to find Jacob as soon as possible, but Sihira was in no situation to listen, but after much pleading she agreed to help her, half heartedly.

As promised Remiri told them the location. Aiden asked Remiri that if she was a helper at the Lab then why were the Lab staff trying to kill her. Remiri replied it was not the work of Ziranso, but of the one who wanted to kill Karan. He also wanted to kill her because she knew the secret composition of the neurotoxin, they used to kill people. "I have been testing the toxins sent to me and have devised a cure for it," she said.

Aiden without wasting another minute asked her for the anti-toxin. She showed him a pen drive and put it back in her pocket saying she would only give it to them if they promised to save her. Aiden told her that he had already agreed to her former condition and he would save her no matter what. Remiri smiled softly and told him that he is a kind guy. Meanwhile Sihira standing next to them was burning with anger. Their next step was to reach Reinese. Aiden found bandage nearby and tied it to Remiri's waist where she had been injured and was bleeding profusely. After this the three of them rushed to the exit. but as soon as Remiri stepped out of the building a car hit her killing her on the spot. Aiden silently crawled and took the pen drive from her pocket, covered Sihira's mouth with his hand preventing her from making any sound and went back into the clinic before anyone could see them.

Chapter 9
RUN, KILL, RUN

The person who had hit Remiri with his vehicle called out for help. He was one of the goons who had come to kill Remiri, Sihira and Karan. Meanwhile he crowded the people near Remiri's body he gestured the other three men behind him to go into the clinic and catch the other two. A crowd formed around Remiri's dead body. Some trying to contact the police while some tried calling the ambulance. Aiden realised that escaping is not an option now, so he decided to fight them. He switched on the music speaker and put it to high volume. He knew that the three men coming in were trained commandos and so it would not be easy to defeat them. To hide the sound of his footsteps, he turned on the speaker. He was hiding in a room with a small opening through the door looking at the three searching for him.

Sihira was hiding at the other end of the clinic in another room. Aiden waited for them to split up and search separately, as that way it would be easy for him to take them on. As Aiden expected the three of them after a brief search decided to search separately to find them faster. One of them came towards the room where Aiden was hiding. As soon as he entered, Aiden took a pair of scissors and stabbed him on his calf. As soon as the commando knelt down Aiden wrapped his hands around his mouth and stabbed him continuously on his neck making him bleed intensely thus resulting in his death.

He closed the door and hid beside it on one side. The second one was calling his friend, meanwhile only the one who was alive responded. They realised that one of them had already embraced death. Now realising the seriousness of the situation they both became alert. The second one saw the speaker inside a room and cautiously walked towards it to switch it off. As he entered the room and was about to switch of the speaker, Aiden who was hiding beside the door kicked him from behind. The commando was fast to respond to it, as soon as he fell down he turned towards Aiden who was about to stab him. He held his hands midway and they started struggling. During the struggle the scissor fell out of Aiden's hand but he was able to free his hands from the commando's grasp. He grabbed the speaker and punched it down on the killer's face until and unless he died. While being hit the killer had screamed for help and the speaker being disconnected and broken started to slow down. Due to this the third commando was able to hear his comrade became stood still in the middle of the clinic, keeping his eyes and ears on full alert. Aiden ran from behind him with a knife to stab him but he alerted by the presence turned around and grabbed Aiden. He punched him hard in his guts that sent him flying. Aiden fell at a distance from the goon and realised that he is the strongest out of all.

The goon took out his gun took a shot at him but Aiden was quick enough to run into the room and close the door. The assailant started to advance slowly towards the room with the gun at the ready.

The door was slightly ajar. Just when he came near, Aiden pounced on him. The gun fell from his hand and as he bent down to pick it up Aiden saw a pencil nearby. He grabbed it. The killer got his gun and aimed it at Aiden. As soon as he shot the bullet Aiden ducked, slid towards him, kicked him on his legs and as the killer lost his balance and started falling, Aiden layed down there with the pencil pointed towards the killer. The killer fell one the pencil that pierced through his lower throat instantly killing him.

Aiden pushed the away the dead body, stood up and went to Sihira, grabbed her hand and ran towards the main gate with her. She told him that the killer who hit Remiri with his car must be at the entrance. Aiden consoled her, "With such a crowd there, he won't try to kill us." They stepped out of the entrance to see Remiri being carried away on a stretcher. The man who had hit her looked at them angrily, but couldn't do anything as the crowd hadn't dispersed till then.

They rushed to Aiden's car and drove away. Sihira saw a box at the back, picked it up, and asked Aiden to open it. He did so without any hesitation. It slipped out of her hands when she saw the beating heart. As soon as it fell off her hands the box locked down on its own.

Aiden picked up the box and put it in the box holder. Before Sihira could speak He looked at her and asked, "Do you see any expression on my face?" She looked at him and saw how calm and composed he was even after killing three men and having a living heart in his car. He told her that he did not feel any happiness, sadness or any other kind of emotion because his heart had been removed from his body.

According to science, hormones produce various emotions in humans, and these hormones gets pumped to various parts of the body through veins and the pumping is done by the heart, thus in his case, he had theorized that because of the absence of his real heart in his body he had lost all his emotions. Therefore, he needed to solve the mystery of the heart he was surviving on now. Aiden hid his theory from her that he is not Karan but someone else who was residing in Karan's body . He told her to connect the pen drive to the control panel of the LCD, in the car. They went through its contents, it contained the composition of the toxin and the antitoxin but what caught their eyes and left them dumbstruck were the pictures of Remiri and Jacob!

Remiri was Jacob's sister. Aiden and Sihira looked at each other. He asked Sihira if she had also lost her heart because she seemed calm and composed just as Aiden even after knowing that Remiri had a family. Sihira said that she would never feel anything for a betrayer but anger. Aiden thought of trying to persuade her that she was still her friend and that she had a family, but decided to ignore all those for now and gave her the address slip given by Remiri and told her to direct him there. He was shocked to see that they had reached Jacob's house. "Are you sure this is the location?" he asked her and she assured him that it was.

Without any second thought they went in and were greeted by Jacob's parents. Aiden had got so many surprises and got so acquainted to the shocks after being reincarnated that now he felt that even if he would have had a real heart he wouldn't be able to be shocked anymore. "So, did you find Jacob? Is he fine?" Were the questions thrown at Aiden by Jacob's parents. Aiden consoled them that he had found him but before bringing him here he wanted to be sure of something. He went to Jacob's room and searched every nook and corner. He found nothing special but saw many articles about a particular businessman.

Aiden ruffled through the papers and saw newspaper articles on Karan's accident some of which were highlighted in red. Aiden went into Jacob's parents' room and searched there also. He found nothing except for a blueprint of the house. After studying the blueprint for a long time he went near one of the switches in Jacob's room and pressed it for a long time.

Suddenly a wall behind the cupboard swung open like a door. Aiden and Sihira went in, walked down the stairs, and saw a lab. He saw many experiments; all stamped and approved by the national ministry of health and sciences. Just then, Aiden heard a voice who spoke, "Hey Karan, at last you found me." Aiden turned around to see a person sitting on a chair in a dark corner of that lab. The person leaned forward and the light illuminated his face, it was none other than Jacob himself. Aiden faked a smile and rushed to hug him. He Rained him with questions like who wanted to kill him and why.

As directed by by Jacob, Aiden and Sihira made themselves comfortable on the chairs and then Jacob gave them another shock of the century by telling them that everything had been planned by Karan's brother, Clave. He had tried to get his hands on Karan's stocks and shares. Aiden asked Jacob why and how did Clave tried to kill him. Jacob suggested they stay quite and listen patiently.

"Clave buys litres of these neurotoxins from Ziranso Lab, illegally. He uses them to kill his enemies without leaving any evidence. After learning about this I contacted the Ziranso Lab for the toxins. They did not give me the name of their biggest customer but did give me some toxins but charged me a lot for it. I tried to use some of it on Clave but he came to know that I had bought some toxins, from the scientists of Ziranso. So, he tried to kill me but I found out that some of my men are actually on Clave's payroll. Therefore, I faked my death."

Aiden nodded and turned to Sihira and spoke to her in a voice loud enough to be heard by Jacob, "He told the whole story truthfully but he wrongly placed the characters." Jacob looked at him surprised and asked him what he was trying to imply. Aiden now stood up, walked towards him and told him to make himself comfortable. Aiden told him to sit down quietly and pointed at him the gun he had taken from the goons at the clinic. "You told your part of the story, now let's hear the true one ; from the one you tried to kill; Me. You buy litres of those neurotoxins from the Ziranso Lab illegally and use the toxins to kill your enemies without leaving behind a trace of evidence. Just then, another businessman, your rival, 'Clave', bought some quantity of those toxins from the Ziranso Lab and when you came to know of it, you feared that many would come to know about this toxin and the government would soon ban it and this could also result in shutting down of the lab, as they worked on those toxins without government's approval. So, you tried to kill him but he survived.

"He tried to kill you by the same method but you knew it already so you used a 3d printer to print a face mask of yourself and made one of your men wear it. And one day that man whom you made your duplicate died from those toxins and then you came to know that you had betrayers working for your rival among your men. You killed those betrayers but you didn't let anyone know that you were still alive. You started working under an anonymous name, but only the people of the lab knew the truth but never tried to expose it because now they were getting double the payment they used to get. Thus, they kept their mouths shut. So the whole truth is now in the open. So you can save us and yourself from the pity acting and answer my last question truthfully; that why did you want to kill me?"

Jacob smiled, "So you don't know why I wanted to kill you?" He stood up, banged his hands on the table, looked into Aiden's eyes, and turned towards Sihira with wrath in eyes to narrate the whole story, "He agreed to help me with the medicine factory project in the slums and I invested in it and made him it's major holder, I had to make him their partner because he had the face value and being one of the greatest businessman they trusted him. When the project was halfway, the slum dwellers came to him requesting that they didn't want to leave their homes even if they were getting better places to live in, and Karan being Karan couldn't handle the emotions of those beggars and agreed to stop the project." He then looked back at Karan with the same anger in his eyes and started narrating the other half, "Not even once you thought about me or asked my opinion and just ordered me to cancel the project.

I had no choice but to agree as you were the major holder of the contractor. I agreed to it and cancelled the project but do you know the loss difference? Due to the cancellation you faced a loss of mere 22 crore rupees but do you know how much I suffered—a total of 1220 crores and the trusts of many investors; may be you were the major percent partner of the work but I was the major investor. After that I was neck deep in debts from banks and other investors, I tried to go back to those people and told them to resume the project without you but no one agreed. That day I realised that Iam nothing without your identity. These thoughts hunted me so much that I was on the verge of killing myself but just then the Ziranso Lab heard about my problem and came to my rescue."

Aiden raised his eyebrows and said, "So you poisoned all your investor with the toxin and then offered them the anti-toxin in exchange for their stocks. Then you got your hands on their stocks, paid back the banks, and tried to kill me in revenge." Jacob angrily hit the table. "And yet you survived. I tried to kill you in a car accident. I also tried to poison you to get your stocks , as in today's market they are valued in billions. But every time you survived and the toxins showed zero effect leaving no space for me to threaten you, but my luck was with me. I got the perfect opportunity to keep you alive and make more money from you rather than from your stocks."

Aiden asked what was the reason that stopped Jacob from killing him. Jacob continued but this time with a wicked smile, "You are the reason for leaving your survival, since your blood was tested and found to be somewhat mutated, that is, it is different from that of normal humans. I thought that your blood could be used as a cure, but not immediately. We would make the toxin a little less lethargic and then spread it like a virus among the people. Once it became pandemic and a national issue, I would demand a large sum of money from the government for the making of the cure and the approval for the Ziranso lab to work independently on whichever project they want without Government's interference. See, originally this was the plan, but you know what was not the plan? You standing here and learning all about this.' Jacob also had a question for him which he asked without any fear, "How did you figure out all of this?"

Still pointing the gun at him, Aiden started speaking, "You really did well in keeping these secrets to yourself, but sitting here you couldn't avoid the mistakes of your men. The day you sent me the note, one of my men called someone and said, "He has got it." If he had called someone else, he would have said, "He has got a note." This indicated he had called someone who already knows about the note and who would know about that note except for the one who sent it. In Remiri's pen drive I saw pictures of her with you and deduced you were her brother. However, I saw her pictures with another man and after seeing the articles about that same man in your room I realised that Remiri had pictures with your rival.

"Another mistake you made was to send those men to kill Remiri. Before killing her they told me they worked for someone whose name they couldn't disclose. But why did the killer want to kill Remiri who was on your side helping them to find the owner of the mutated blood sample. Then I realised she was being watched and that she had discovered that you were behind all this. You had to kill her as Remiri was your rival's lover. She did not use her surname and she lived in that clinic rather than in this house, which meant she had a bitter relationship with you. Moreover, one of the men you sent to kill her was the one I had seen when I first came to your house after getting your note. Your parents were not being watched by anyone but we were being watched by you and your men, You really played well but see what did it bring you to; your death. This is your end, Jacob."

He was about to pull the trigger when Sihira stopped him and told him to give him a painful death rather than killing him instantly. Aiden couldn't understand why was she wishing for such a gory thing but seeing a wicked smile spreading on her face he barred himself from asking that question. This was the same smile she had when she saw Remiri being hit by the car. Looking at Aiden's face Sihira realised that she had made a mistake, so to counter it she said "I want him to die the same painful death as Remiri." Aiden knew that this was not the reason but rather than focusing on her he decided to focus on his promise that he had made to

Jacob's parents that he would bring him alive back to them. Aiden lowered the gun. Jacob saw an opportunity and took a piece of plywood kept on a nearby table and hit it hard on Aiden's hand. The gun fell away from Aiden's hands and he was pushed back, Aiden was taken by surprise when suddenly Jacob ran towards him and hit him hard on his guts, Aiden fell down, writhing in pain. Jacob started crying, "You think I didn't know all this? I had already deduced this as one of the possibility so when I heard your voice in my house I had informed the police that Iam alive and had crafted a little story that you are the one who tried to kill me and I was hiding from you. Now that my million-dollar plan is dumped, I can't risk my life so, you have to go to jail my friend."

Jacob was about to leave when Aiden grabbed his legs and pulled him down. Aiden said, "If I kill you now, the police will think I killed you as you had sent them my location and I would be put behind bars, but don't worry I will find a way of surviving all this once I kill you."

Saying this, he wrapped his hands around Jacob's neck trying to snap it., but Jacob keeping his neck stiff was still holding on to the piece of play was about to plunge it into Aiden's chest when suddenly there was sound of bullet leaving the gun and everything went silent. Sihira shot Jacob with the gun that got thrown out of Aiden's hands. Aiden checked his pulses and realised that he is dead, but the bullet wasn't the one that killed him. Jacob got distracted by the bullet's sound in turn leaving his body a little relax that allowed Aiden to snap his neck. He took the gun from Sihira's hands and carried Jacob out of the den. He took him to his parents and told them to take him to the hospital immediately as he had been seriously injured. An ambulance arrived and he was immediately taken to the hospital. Aiden watched them taking

Jacob to the hospital as he told Sihara to send all the contents of the pen drive and any proof present in that room that proves that Jacob was the one behind all this to the police as soon as possible. After doing that they left for the hospital.

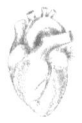

Chapter 10
AIDEN?

The heavy pressure that broke Jacob's neck had also clotted the blood in that region. He was soon operated on and the doctor informed that Jacob had gone into a coma. Jacob's parents broke out into tears while Aiden patted the doctor and said, "Good, now he won't have to go to prison." Aiden told the truth to Jacob's parents. At first, the pain of Jacob's coma and knowing that the one they trusted is the one who sent their son into coma, really shocked them. They couldn't say anything, they were shocked to their very core, they stood there as if frozen. Seeing them unable to apprehend or reply Aiden shouted to the doctor.

The doctor took them into the treatment ward. Sihira blamed Aiden, "How can you do this to them, Karan?" Aiden just apologised to her and told her that being parents they had to learn the truth. Saying this he said that they had to leave now as the problem had yet to be solved. Both of them drove off. Sihira asked him where they were going. Aiden said they were now going to find Clave and find out why he had tried to save them.

Aiden remembered that he had completely forgotten about his own problems and was working on making Karan's life better. He reached Clave's house and asked the guard if they could meet him. He replied that he did not stay at home much, so he can't say definitely at what time they could meet him. He could not say where he was, as he keeps on wandering from place to place without informing anyone.

While Aiden was returning, he got a call from an unknown number. He picked it up, but before he could say anything, the caller spoke, "So you have come to me at last." He told Aiden where he can meet him and hung up. Aiden checked his phone and saw he had got forty-two missed calls from Vaahindi. He returned home and told him all that had happened. "So you had been working for Clave, right?" Vaahindi smiled and nodded saying that he would know the truth once he will meet him.

Aiden and Sihira sat down to have some food. Vaahindi from the start never liked Sihira and even Karan had promised never to meet her again, but Aiden till date couldn't understand the reason behind it as she thought her to be a nice girl with a liking towards Karan. Vaahindi served him food meanwhile ordered one of the other servants to serve food to Sihira. While they were having their food Vaahindi gave her a stern and hateful look. Sihira just reciprocated with a smile. Aiden could feel the tension so he finished his food as fast and possible and also told her to do the same. The butler wanted to tell him why Karan had left her but never got an appropriate place or time to tell him and before he could tell her they left. They reached the place they were told, there they saw a house; a two storey building built on a barren land with no lawns and few neighbours. They entered to see six men at dinner. Aiden recognised one of them as Clave from the pictures he had seen at Jacob's house. Clave spoke, "So, Aiden."

Aiden was surprised to hear the name from him, but he realised that Karan's butler is working for him which means if the butler knows the truth then so does Clave. He noticed someone else was also shocked. Sihira did not know what was going on so she asked,

"Aiden? Who is Aiden? Aren't you Karan?" Aiden told her to calm down and then sat alongside her on a sofa nearby. He was calm and composed and waited for Clave to finish eating.

Clave and the others came and sat down near them. Aiden asked him how he knew he was not Karan. Clave replied, "Can't a brother know this? From the day you re-lived, you have never asked about me and always kept saying that you are Aiden and not Karan. Your actions did not resemble even one per cent of my brother's and we knew you were being watched so we tried our best to divert the people from the fact that Karan's body had been taken over by someone else.

"That's the reason Vaahindi told you how Karan found new ideas for his books. I told him to say so that Karan usually acts as one of the characters of his books so as to get new ideas inspired from real life. We had to say as we were being constantly watched. I also tried saving Remiri but before I could send my men, she had already been killed. We would have killed Jacob but we couldn't find his hideout and then we realised that whoever you are inside Karan's body, you are a clever fellow so we just focused on protecting you and let you solve the mystery."

Aiden nodded and asked him who Karan was and why he had been transferred to his body. Clave resumed his narration. "Karan was my brother and was a kind of immortal guy; he would only die at a particular age, that is 70 but can also be killed before that by weapons, even if his heart was torn out of his body he would still live. His heart is indestructible. Only at a desired time, desired place and by a chosen weapon can he be killed. After death he gets reborn again with all memories of past life, I took birth as his brother in this life but Iam no immortal and a normal human The one characteristic that is noticeable in Karan is his extreme sensitiveness. Once I was hurt from falling from cycle and seeing my pain he also started crying. We cried for a long time. I thinking him a weak man told him that he couldn't protect his younger brother. He stopped crying and told me 'Yes you are right, I couldn't protect any of my family, neither you nor any of my other brothers in my other lives.' Listening this I stopped crying and blaming him, but he didn't say anything about this any further."

"The Aiden's family you have been trying to find —I couldn't find your family but did investigate about Aiden Ermish and found that he had died four years ago. I guessed your soul had been preserved in your real body and the day Karan's heart was taken you were placed in his." Saying this, Clave handed him a photo of the real Aiden and asked him if he was the same person.

Aiden nodded and said, "Who was the one who had preserved his soul for four years and transferred it to Karan's body and why was that done?". Clave shook his head indicating he did not know. Aiden thought it better to keep the heart a secret from them as while trying to get his brother back, Clave might transplant Karan's heart in his body in turn reviving Karan and killing Aiden. As he was lost in such thoughts, he heard cars screeching to a halt outside. They peeped out of the window and saw that some men in black suits had surrounded the house.

Aiden looked at Clave and asked, "So you too have enemies?" Clave smiled and replied they were not his enemies but had come to get Karan. Aiden exclaimed, "How many enemies did your brother have?" Clave smiled and said "Thousands, but don't worry these are Jacob's men. As he was in a coma, his family was still paying the men. They will try to avenge their master and therefore followed you to kill you."

Aiden asked how they could escape as the men had guns. Aiden looked at the five men Clave was having dinner with. They too were scared but listening to Clave's order they walked out of the door one by one. Jacob's men were astonished to see five unarmed men walking out of the house. The twelve of them were ready with their fingers on the triggers. They walked up to the five men checked for any weapons on them and then started questioning them. However, those five walked to the car and sat in it.

Clave was counting backwards from ten.

Aiden was observing Clave's behaviour and that of the five men in the car. Before he could ask anything, Clave took out his mobile and started counting, "One, two, three, four, and five." Saying this, he pressed five buttons. There were five consecutive blasts outside. He realised those five were suicide bombers.

Clave said, "Let's escape now as there are many more that would come. This place is not safe anymore." The three of them were about to drive away in Clave's car when Aiden remembered something and told Clave that he would go in his own car. Clave agreed and gave him some guns and ammunition. Aiden looked at Sihira questioningly to know with whom she would go with. She was silent.

Clave broke the silence, "Let's all go in your car." They rushed to it and drove away. Clave drove while Aiden and Sihira sat at the back. Aiden started a conversation with Clave. "How can you kill your own men to save yourself?" Clave replied, "Oh! They were not my men. I don't drag my men into this mess and that's why I always travel alone to this farmhouse as this is where I plan all the dirty work, like killing my enemies or destroying their business and life. Of the five who died, four were major investors in the neurotoxin. They had collaborated with me to provide funds to the Ziranso Lab to produce that toxin. I had to kill them to stop the spread of the toxin. The fifth man was the head of the project. I blackmailed him to destroy all the data about the neurotoxin. He was the only one who knew how to make it and so I had to kill him, I had to do nothing, I had planted explosives inside of them. I knew you would finally come to meet me and Jacob's men will surely follow you so it was just a counter measure."

Aiden realised that Karan's brother was an intelligent beast who defeated his opponents strategically. Then he turned to Sihira and said, "I know I have deceived you but keeping quiet is not the way to solve it. Please speak your heart out. I will accept your feelings; don't avoid the topic like this." Sihira did not reply and chose to be silent.

The thing that amused him was that she had not revealed about the heart to Clave. They stopped at a restaurant to have some food and rest for the night. Clave received a call and he warned Aiden and Sihira to be on the lookout as the police was also searching for them.

They stopped at Clave's house. Aiden followed Clave into his room and told him that he had many questions that were bothering him. Clave told him to sit down and calmly ask him one by one and that he would try his best to answer them satisfactorily. Aiden started by asking how and why he had been transferred to his brother's body and whether he knew anything about the cursed tale that killed the one who narrated it. He also wanted to know how he had died four years ago and what Karan's brother actually was.

Clave listened to the questions, poured some drinks, and offered some to Aiden, but Aiden refused. Clave took a sip and started answering. "I do not know why your soul was transferred to my brother's body. It is a mystery for me. I have also not heard of the cursed tale you mentioned. However, what you have said about it is beyond human imagination. It is something I have never heard of earlier."

As for how Aiden had died four years ago, Clave searched and found that he was an orphan who lived all by himself, did two to three odd jobs to survive, and died due to kidney failure. He was twenty-one years old at the time of his death and was buried by the orphanage. His life was not so significant as he had lived and died a normal life, so why his soul was transferred into Karan's body is the greatest question.

"Last but not the least, my brother was an immortal who could neither be killed nor die of any disease his cells were highly active and wounds on his body would heal in seconds, even the deadliest of cancer virus were cured in his body. Cuts and broken parts would grow back, there was only one way, that is ' a desirable place, at a desirable time, with a desirable weapon' about which no one knows except for Karan.. He was a human hydra, and we also used to imagine out of curiosity that if he was to cut in half vertically, each half would grow back thus turning into two Karans, but he never let us try it. He used to tell us about his immortality but never spoke how or from where he got it."

He always used to speak of the Dreeknians and how they fought to protect their own people and that their unity is something to be learnt by the whole world. Every time we asked him to tell us more, he would become quiet. He wrote many books and most of them were related to the Dreek nation, and its kings.

"We could never know if the stories were true or fiction but we were sure of one thing that he was related to the Dreeknians. He warned us against visiting Dreek saying it would be dangerous for us. We would ask him to come with us but he would become sad and say he could never ever face the Dreeknians again in his life.

"One day, we were frustrated about these puzzling details about him and asked him to tell us the truth about his life and immortality. That's when we came to know that Karan could only be killed by any Dreeknians old armoury weapon or could die of old age before he was born again. Before he could tell us more, he got a call from his office and rushed away.

"That was the last time we had seen him. His heart was stolen and according to what he had said, he is immortal and his body can only die when his heart is taken away but once it's replaced, he would live again. We found his heartless body and carried it home, took care of the wounds, placed an artificial heart, stitched the hole in his chest. However, we were shocked the next day when his body woke up and we realised it was not Karan, rather the soul was of somebody else.

"We started searching for Karan's heart and that's how we reached his killer. We realised that Jacob didn't know anything about Karan's immortality and he had only tried to kill because of business rivalry. So, there was some unknown entity working against Karan and that unknown entity could be the one who transferred you into my brother's body. That is all I know; for more answers you will have to talk to my brother. Unfortunately, we don't' have his heart so we have to keep searching for it."

Aiden heard Clave patiently but yet he could not trust him with Karan's heart. He had already seen what kind of a demon Clave was. He would place the heart inside his body as soon as he got it, that in turn would revive his brother and kill Aiden. So Aiden kept the secret of the heart to himself. He left and went to Sihira's room. He entered and Sihira asked him what he wanted.

He hugged her tightly, looked into her eyes and said, "May be I don't have feelings, maybe I am not the one you have loved, but believe me no one understands your pain more than me, and I am sure the day I regain my feelings, I will learn about my true feelings for you." Saying this, he turned to leave, but Sihira grabbed his hand and told him to stay with her tonight as she was scared to sleep alone because of all that had happened. He was the only one she could trust as he was the one who had protected her till now. "I don't care if you have feelings or not, but the one I love is you and you may be Karan or Aiden, I don't care; the one thing I do know is that you tried to protect me even if you yourself were in danger. So, I am not going to leave you ever."

Images of his mother and Yelena whom he had tried to protect flashed through Aiden's mind, he remembered his time with them. Now, he did not know how and where they were. Coming back to reality, He hugged Sihira, promising to protect her always and that he would never let her go.

Aiden wanted to learn more about Karan, so this time he asked Sihira about how she had met Karan and what kind of a human being was he. He had heard about him from others but he wanted to know her opinion. He hoped to get some information about Karan from her that could be helpful in his quest. He thought that in most cases, people share their secrets with their lover rather than with family, friends, and colleagues.

Sihira began relating all that she knew about Karan while Aiden listened eagerly.

Chapter 11

OBSESSION OR INSANITY?

Sihira started narrating her story. "I was one of the editors Karan hired for his book production company. He had his own fan base in his company. All the workers were his fans except for the chief editor, John Kelsey. John was a weird guy, and weird in the sense he loved him, or you can say obsessed with him, in fact so obsessed that he wanted to marry Karan and live with him for ever but Karan was not that kind of person. Rather he was 'straight' and interested in the opposite gender.

"He would often ignore John's love signals and rather accept it as friendly vibes, but John never stopped his advances. He constantly dropped hints like keeping roses for him on his table and winking at him. Many of the staff knew about this secret crush but no one dared to mention it to Karan because after all he was 'our boss'.

"No doubt. Karan was a cheerful and lenient guy , while the staff kept quiet about Kelsey, Karan was already aware about it but did nothing to stop it. The staff also never tried to tease or taunt him thinking it might hurt his ego. John's obsession increased day by day and to a limit where he couldn't accept Karan's ignorance anymore. However, he was afraid to speak openly to him. So, He devised a plan. Karan's next book was a multi-million project. Seeing the widespread and heavy sales of his books, a large company, LAPA, decided to produce a film on one of his books.

"Many other producers had tried earlier to persuade Karan to work with them but he would refuse them as he believed in reading books as the true collection of knowledge but this time, he accepted as LAPA offered a huge sum that couldn't be refused. So Karan promised a masterpiece for the film. After he completed the book, John forced me and the other three editors to edit it as soon as possible.

"This was when I began doubting John. He was a person who loved to take time to complete a work without any flaws but this time he wanted it be done quickly. As soon as he received the edited copy, he didn't even read it, he just thanked us and told us that something big is coming our way. We became happy thinking that he may be talking about the film that was going to be released, so we didn't question him, but something wasn't right. He always reads the book after being edited so as to remove even the most minimal mistake, but this time he didn't.

"I thought something was fishy because He always reads the book after being edited so as to remove even the most minimal mistake, but this time he didn't. I started following him, and realised he was in contact with the people of LAPA and without proofreading sent the copy to them. In fact he was the one who persuaded Karan to allow one of his books to be converted into a movie or Karan would have never accepted the deal as he was a 'stick to his principles' kind of person. John and LAPA had planned that John would submit the edited manuscript to LAPA as soon as possible and at a much lower price than what Karan was going to get. This would be done before Karan could release the book. LAPA would release the book under the company's name, and then it would be published by Karan rendering him liable to be accused of plagiarism and face defamation.

"Making that an excuse, they would take over all the works of Karan. This was their plan to take over Karan's company. I thought John did it all to take out his frustration on Karan as he never understood his feelings for him. But John had an ulterior motive. He had devised Karan's downfall but also a way for his own rise. Once LAPA got their hands on all Karan's assets Karan would be bankrupt.

"Then John would reach out to help him with the money he received from LAPA, use it to hire the best of lawyers, and would show Karan that he was working hard to collect evidence against LAPA and would produce the evidence after some days of pretending to search to help Karan win the case.

"By doing this Karan would be forever be grateful to John and this opportunity would be a key point for John to propose to him; Karan would not be able to refuse because he would feel he indebted to him. I found out about this great plan and told Karan about it with photographs and videos of John and LAPA's cooperation.

"Soon after John was fired from the company and I was promoted as the chief editor. However, that was not the end as John thought that I had done all this to draw Karan's attention towards myself. He didn't realise that I did it to save the company, because once a company gets defamed it can never gain back it's reputation as it used to have, thus leading to the downfall of the company. To take revenge, he planned to defame me and the company. He first committed some heinous crimes against the company starting from protests to paying newspapers to print false news about Karan and his organisation. Karan after such baseless defamation filed another case, requested the court to exile John from the country.

"The court seeing all the evidences and proves accepted his plea and ordered John to leave the country and never enter Milatintia again. After that, John set his real plan in action by starting a nightmarish life for me. John's people here in Milatintia attacked me everywhere I went. There were knife attacks or late night knocking on my door.

"I complained to Karan that John had not left the country. I hadn't realised that the ones scaring me wasn't John himself, rather it was his men who were in the country trying to scare me and make my life hell. Karan sent some of his men to Abhitipoz, the country where John lived, to keep an eye on him. Meanwhile, the attacks against me continued. Karan tried to make me understand that his men were constantly keeping an eye on John who was working as an editor at a small publishing company.

"When he got frustrated by my constant complaining, he declared me insane. The next day, while working on a new book, I looked out of the window and saw John. I jumped out of my chair and started screaming and throwing things out of the window. Karan was observing me along with some workers of the mental hospital. They saw me in that situation and thought I had some psychological problem and admitted me to a mental hospital. Medication and electric shocks were forced on me, life became hell for me.

"I made some friends at the asylum, including the staff who helped me escape from that hell. One of them had parked a scooty outside the hospital. While I rode away, someone on my way to my house threw acid on me. I dodged it but slipped and was hit by a truck. That is when you showed up and helped me. Since then, you have helped and stayed with me. I realised you were not the Karan I knew. So, I stuck to you as you were the one who could help. As expected, no one came to take me back to that hell again. Therefore, I request you to stay with me for ever."

After completing her story, Sihira looked at him while Aiden was in deep thought. She started speaking to break the silence.

"Hello, Aiden are you listening?"

"Huh! Yes, Yes! So where is the love in this love story?"

"I never said it was a love story."

"It's not so much of an epic love story; rather it was a horror one."

Saying this Aiden sighed, and then comforted her to sleep. He came out and slowly closed the door behind him, leaned against the wall and started talking, but this time not to himself rather with the one standing there already; Clave.

"So, do you have any proof that she is mentally unstable?"

"I can show you pics and videos we clicked of her secretly."

"Pictures! like?"

"Pictures of her being scared by John or attacked by him."

Clave showed him the pictures and asked,

"Do you see anyone else in this video?"

"No."

"But still, she is screaming as if a ghost is haunting her."

"So how can we treat her?"

"The doctors said that it is a type of schizophrenic disorder and there is no treatment; she can only improve when left near her loved ones."

"So, I keep her mind at peace, but I want to know how come she became like this?"

"She used to hate and fear John a lot; hate as she wanted the chief editor's position and fear of his knowledge and cleverness. She always looked for an opportunity to get him kicked out of the company; she was the one who worked with LAPA and blamed it all on John. Karan believed her and fired John. Before leaving John threatened her that he would destroy her life. Being already scared of him, this threat by John became a nightmare for her. Before John could harm her, he was exiled but his fear still remains with her

"Meanwhile, Karan, instead of comforting her during her nightmare did not pay much attention to her and that triggered her fear still more till the point that she was declared insane and was sent to the mental hospital. There her condition worsened as you can see in this video while escaping from the asylum there was no acid attack on her; she just imagined there was someone attacking her and dodged in such a manner that she was hit by a truck."

Aiden listened to him and then told him that it was not the truth. Clave seemed confused and asked what he was trying to imply. Aiden told him, "Maybe she is scared of John at present, but her obsession with Karan was from childhood. Her mother died at a young age due to a chronic heart disease. She was just two years old and thus her father had to marry again so that someone could stay at home to take care of Sihira while he goes to office. Her step-mother loved and cared for her but for a limited period of time. She soon had her child and thus started neglecting Sihira, Sihira saw how her mother always stuck to her son and took care of him. This was the initial point of the start of her madness. That was the time when Karan met her for the first time. She was eleven at that time He saw how Sihira was neglected, and sympathised her. They grew close both physically and emotionally. He would take her out and spend time with her till the evening.

However, as soon as Karan was successful in his life and career, he felt some mysterious person was between them, like some other person standing between his emotions and Sihira telling him to distance himself from her. He wanted to spend time with Sihira but felt she was an obstacle between him and that mysterious person. Thus his feelings for started fading away and he started ignoring her; Being neglected during her childhood the only true care and love she got is from Karan and thus being neglected also by him gave her a trauma and her madness that was started by her stepmother was ignited further, thats when Sihira's obsession changed to insanity; This insanity stayed with her till she started working at karan's publishing company and the John's incident took place that just worked as a spark for that inflammable fuel."

Clave looked at him shocked, and asked how he knew all this. Aiden sighed and told him that he had done a few investigations on her and now Clave's story and proves added up to his results to give out the final conclusion. He did not reveal his powers to Clave. Clave asked in a tensed tone if he was falling in love with her. Aiden looked at him expressionless and replied with a question, "Do I look like I feel anything?"

Clave looked at his lifeless face and told him he should never even think of loving someone without Karan's permission. Also, he should not love anyone at all as he was leading someone else's life and soon the body will be taken over by its original owner. So, he should avoid any kind of physical and emotional use of the body without Karan's permission.

Aiden said that the one who lived is the one who ruled; that's what survival of the fittest is all about. "We need to be a little selfish so as to survive, and unless your brother gets back into this body, it is my responsibility to take care of it and how it is used. You cannot say anything on this; and about Sihira, I can't say that I may love her but Iam sure that I will protect her. This is not because I love her and am also sure even after getting back my feelings I am not going to feel any love for her. I just want to support her out of sympathy, I don't want her to feel neglected anymore.'

Saying this Aiden told him to wake up early and get ready as nowhere was safe for a long period as Rivet's men would be following them and reach there soon. They went to sleep. It was a restless night but the only one who slept peacefully was Sihira as she felt protected and safe with Aiden nearby. He realised how a fear instilled in a human can take him/her to the verge of mental instability.

He promised himself that he would not give another reason for Sihira to fear. But even after all this, he felt empty. He was just acting on instinct by the way of humanity to help others, to redeem his sins from his past life. But the truth was he was not feeling any compassion or love towards anything or anyone.

The three of them woke up in the morning and got ready and were about to leave when the receptionist persuaded them to stay for breakfast. They refused but the receptionist was insistent. Hearing the commotion, the other workers and the manager arrived at the spot. Clave complained about the poor service of the hotel and the receptionist's bad behaviour. The manager apologised and insisted that they at least have breakfast before leaving "The breakfast will be on us sir, an expression of gratitude from our hotel to our unsatisfied customers."

Aiden suspected something fishy and tried to talk to Clave but Sihira could not resist her hunger and rushed to the dining room and jumped on the food.

Chapter 12

THE DEATH BOUNDARY

Aiden realised that they had been tricked. Seeing no way to escape, he acted as if he knew nothing and went to their room along with Clave. He told Clave, "They are Jacob's men. They must have been ordered to stall us till Rivet arrives with his men. Therefore, they won't let us leave. They must have been offered a huge sum to catch us alive thus they are not trying to kill us. As for Jacob's parents, they don't need any information from us which means they just want to give us a slow and painful death in front of their son. Therefore, we have to escape from here as soon as possible."

Clave was confused. The hoodlums had surrounded the building waiting for Jacob's parents to arrive. Aiden told him to calm down, "Yesterday night, after talking to you, I checked the blueprint of the hotel in their office." Clave was confused as to how he entered the office room as it is exclusively for staffs to access. Aiden said he bribed the guard and entered to check out the blueprint structure for a situation like this. "I had suspected that they were trapping us. Thus I have already devised a plan after checking out the hotel's blueprint."

They called Sihira and went into Clave's bathroom where Aiden removed a section of the drainage pipe. The pipe led directly to the city drainage system and opened to the manhole on main road. They escaped through it but where they emerged from it

Two snipers were there on the roof of opposite building aiming at them. Aiden had earlier seen them through his window while leaving the hotel. Knowing that they were there, Aiden just raised the lid up but did not slide it aside.

Each sniper shot once and stopped. Aiden checked through the peephole of the manhole and saw the snipers leaving. Aiden gestured the other two, they came out of the man hole and rushed to their car and as soon as they started it, they realised the snipers' shots had alerted the hotel's security who were coming for them. They drove off as fast as they could but It was not the end.

The security men started chasing them in their cars. Aiden had already planned where to go. Clave and Sihira kept asking him where they were going and how they would survive.

Clave suggested he call his men to come and protect them but Aiden turned him down and said he did not want to involve any innocents in their troubles and it would have been too late for them to arrive. Clave tried to argue, "We are paying them to protect us and...." Before he could complete his sentence, he saw Aiden staring at him with anger in his eyes, so he kept quiet. Many a time they had changed direction and stopped to rest and eat. They know this peace would not last long.

They drove as fast as they could and reached to the so-called 'death boundary'. As they came out of the car and stood at the boundary they heard cars driving towards them. Clave cried "Do we really have to enter it?" To which Aiden replied "We have no other choice." Clave thought it better to learn about the mystery before dying so he followed Aiden and sihira followed both of them. The security, goons and Jacob's parents did not follow them because they knew it was called the death boundary for a reason. Aiden had seen in Karan's memory how speeding objects that tried to enter the boundary were burned down to ash. He walked in while one or two cars who tried to follow were consumed by fire as soon as they entered.

Aiden had never seen inside the boundary in Karan's memory. It was as if Karan had set up a wall against the memories inside the boundary so that no one can ever access them, but now he saw how beautifully the Dreeks had developed themselves; It was the country of Dreek; a mystery searched by many but solved by none. Yes, the Dreek country boundary is called the 'death boundary' because no one has every returned alive from there once they went into it. So those trying to capture him turned back even spurning the amount of 5,000 pounds to bring him back dead or alive.

After crossing the boundary, Clave and Sihira were scared thinking they would soon die. Clave accused Aiden, "You are immortal, but we are not and now we will die, still young and in the prime of health, while you will live for ever." Aiden ignored him and walked forward with Sihira. She was clinging to him ever since they had crossed. All eyes were on them.

Even Aiden was not sure if they would survive or not. They were shocked to see the development, they had large energy resources and they also filtered and use ocean water as drinking water, they had machineries that had efficiency to use solar energy to its fullest extent and many more. They saw a large statue of a person with a double-sided sword at the entrance of the boundary. Just then, some of Jacob's hoodlums followed Aiden's steps and walked across. They took out their guns to shoot at them. Aiden tried to protect Sihira and Clave but before they could shoot, many more guns were aimed at them. The hoodlums got scared and surrendered. They were taken away by the country police.

Aiden and his friends were taken in by some people and imprisoned. The three of them discussed about the Dreeknians who were so developed, much ahead than the rest of the world and how they had developed their science and culture equally? They were dressed as earlier Dreeknians used to, in the primeval times. There were forests and greenery everywhere. Cleanliness was also emphasised, one could not see any dirt or refuse anywhere.

Aiden tried to talk to the jailor who guarded them but they were strictly prohibited from talking to the prisoners.

The next day they were taken to the court and without any questioning they were awarded death sentences. The three of them were shocked. Clave protested that the court had no right to sentence them without even listening to them. Besides, their crime should be told to them. But his protests fell on deaf ears and they were locked up again.

This time, the new jailor was a talkative one. Aiden asked him why even after being a type-2 civilisation, humans in here are still working on their own, like sweeping the roads, cleaning toilets and etc, rather than using robots or hi-tech machineries. He replied that the Dreek government had decreed that humans should never stop working as total dependence on robots and machines would make them lazy and slow the process of development. Robots and machines can't develop new ideas and imagination like humans thus declining the process of development, and once the humans become dependant on robots and machineries they become too lazy even to think of new ideas.

He said that Dreek is far different from all other countries and that even after so much development they were not allowed to share it with the outer world. They valued their culture as it was taught to them by their kings and they worshipped God and respected their scriptures. They were different from the rest of the world, they follow only their own religion. They all follow the same religion so there is no conflict either on the basis of religion or of region.

Thus, they have saved their manpower, revenue, and assets for united development. Aiden asked him how they had achieved such advancements. The jailor said it was all due to the Supreme who had blessed them with this development.

After some conversation, and becoming friendly with the jailor, Aiden bribed him to let them go. The jailor started talking with them without looking at them so that the security watching the cctv would think that the jailor is talking to themselves. The jailor merely gestured to show them how they could escape. Thus, the camera would show his movements were natural.

After some time, he acted as if he fell asleep and Aiden reached out his arm and took the keys from his pocket, for such developed country the prisons were pretty primitive. He opened the lock and escaped with Sihira and Clave. On his way, he saw other cells surrounded by glass on all sides to keep a constant watch on the inmates. The jailor woke up and deliberately ran after them after they had already escaped. The alarm blared and the officers and staff were alerted.

The three of them realised they had no way to escape from Dreek and that they were powerless to fight against the Dreeknians. As they had lost all their hopes just then a car came up and the door opened inviting them in. A girl was driving it. She told the three of them to tie their seat belts as she sped off. Clave was about to question her when she told him not to say anything till they reach their destination.

They went into a jungle where a tree trunk opened like a door and she drove in. Inside was a cavernous hollow in which many people were working, sleeping, eating, or reading. It was like a country in its own.

Aiden and his friends were taken to a room where they saw the same jailor who had helped them escape. Aiden walked up to him and gave him the money he had promised. The jailor returned it. Before Aiden could ask anything, he told him to wait for the head to come. They could then talk freely to clear their doubts.

Clave tried to protest but Aiden shushed him and told him to be patient. They sat and waited. After some hours, they were given food and were told to

rest as they must be tired from their escape. Aiden told Sihira and Clave that if they needed to survive, they would have to obey orders as the people who had brought them there had no intention to hurt them.

They ate to their fill and went to sleep, but the problem was that there was no bed. The only thing they saw were switches on the wall.

Clave switched one them on. Fans and lights protruded out of the walls. A television set and mobiles, air-conditioner and even beds came out of the floor. The three were surprised by the advanced technology but they were too tired to praise the developments. So, they just went to sleep.

The jailor came in the morning to wake them up as the head had arrived. The head was a beautiful young lady. She entered, turned off the bed switches and other unnecessary ones, the Dreeknians were strict o the use of resources. They believed in using the necessity and conserving the rest. She told them to get ready in an hour. They got ready in an hour and went to speak to the head.

She started the conversation, "So Karan, Clave and Sihira, I am Celly. You have been sentenced to death but we protected you for a reason. We are anti-nationals, that is, we are in the favour of the king." Meanwhile, Clave and Sihira concentrated on her talks, Aiden was smiling as he realised why Karan felt a barrier between him and Sihira. It was because he had never loved Sihira. Celly ignoring their expressions was about to continue but Clave interrupted her with a question, "Aren't anti-nationals those, who are against the king or the government?"

Celly replied, "In this country, nationalists refer to the ones against the King and the anti-nationals are the one who support the present government and hate the king; Not the present king rather we are divided on the basis of support on our past king named Karan. Those who support him are anti-nationalists. It is we who saved our king, Karan, and its none other than you. We know you may not remember your past. Therefore, we intend to remind you and send you on a mission to save the lives of millions of people. You have two choices; either die at the hands of the government, or complete the mission and live as free men."

Chapter 13

KARAN

Celly told them that they have one hour to decide as there was not much time to waste, and left them. Aiden told the other two not to reveal the truth that he was living in Karan's body as they might think them useless and kill them. Both of them agreed and decided that they would go on the mission and alongside find an escape route. They called the head in and told her that they were ready to go on the mission but before that they have some conditions. Celly agreed to listen to them. With a gloomy expression and deep voice Aiden enumerated them. "First, you have to ensure that the government will waive our death sentence; second, you need to protect us from any potential threat that they may pose to us; third, give us a contract in writing that after the mission is accomplished, you won't kill us or harm us in any way and would let us live as free men."

Celly patiently listened to the conditions and guaranteed them the last two. As for the first, it was in the government's hands so they were helpless. However, they would do their best to protect them from the government spies. The three of them were reluctant at first but seeing no other option they nodded and began preparing for the mission. The first step was to make Karan remember his past as the Dreeknians did not know that it was Aiden's soul that was in Karan's body. As far as the anti-nationalists were concerned, they believed that Karan is working with them.

They tried to make Karan remember his past. Sihira told them that he had acquired the power of knowing the secrets of something or someone just by touching it or them. As Sihira started the sentence Aiden realised that she was about to reveal his secrets but before he could stop her, she blurted out the whole sentence. Aiden realised that he is in deep trouble now, he just looked at her and gave her a death stare. Celly, curious about this new discovery, rained him with questions like where he had acquired this power and how frequently could he use it. Aiden told them that he could not use this power properly as he is not in control of that power and did not know the source of that power.

As soon as he completed his sentence, four men pounced on him and cuffed him to a nearby chair. Clave was having his lunch when he heard the commotion and rushed into the room. He looked at the situation and thought Aiden's secret was out. To save themselves, he rushed to help him out. Clave was awfully stronger than normal humans. As Aiden had thought, Clave is truly a beast. He was able to take down two of them at a time, but before he could continue, he was tasered by Celly rendering his movements. He pleaded the head, "We also didn't know that he is Aiden. We stayed with him because we thought he is Karan; he has deceived us for such a long time. Karan is my brother and this girl here, Sihira, is her lover. So please don't hurt that body. Even Aiden is helpful to us. He can help you complete whatever your mission is."

Clave cried for some time and then realised there was no reply. He looked up and saw Celly's face. It was a face of shock and frustration. He looked at Aiden who stared at him hopelessly and thus he realised his mistake. Aiden was still expressionless but realised they were in deep trouble. Celly angrily asked them, "How many more secrets are you hiding from us. You never had any intention to complete the mission. All you wanted was to escape as soon as you got the chance."

On Celly's orders two men pointed their guns at Sihira and Clave. Celly told Aiden, "Tell us the truth or they won't live." Celly still did not see any worry on Aiden's face and thought he did not care about them. While Celly was still thinking, Aiden spoke, "Think about it; once you kill them you won't be able to force me to complete the mission. So, tell your men to put down their guns and I would tell you everything about Karan and me."

Aiden related everything about his past life and the cursed tale and how he made a deal with the Devil to wipe out humans, but he realised that the Devil wanted their life energy to revive his own army of demons. So, he had signed another deal to stop the curse but in exchange his existence would be wiped out and people would no longer remember Aiden.

However, the devil played some dirty game and, he put Aiden in another body. and Aiden did not know why and how he had ended up in the body of Karan who was immortal and who could heal the most severe injuries in minutes. He also said how Karan's memory and life energy is captured in his heart which he has with him

All of them were shocked and this time even Clave was left with a clueless expression and asked what Aiden was trying to say. He replied, "Yes, I have hidden it till now and even Sihira do know this. Actually, I tried to research about this immortal person and came to know that Karan lives on inside his heart as he can't be killed by regular weapons or poison; which means when I was being transferred into that body, he was still alive. Now the questions arise; why did Karan transferred his consciousness into his heart?

This leads to three conclusions that either Karan knew beforehand about the accident and just before it he had transferred his life energy and consciousness to his heart thinking it would remain alive or he was tired of his immortality and living in this mortal world thus, transferred his life into his heart, last but not the least somehow, he was manipulated by the devil and got trapped inside his own heart.

Celly asked him where he had hidden the card to which Aiden took a knife from one of the guards. They tried to aim their guns thinking that Aiden may try to hurt them but Aiden gestured them to calm down and slowly tore one side of his stomach, took out a card and gave it to Celly. The heart was kept inside the converted card, that used to be a box; Aiden had pushed the card into his stomach when he was caught by the Dreeknians. Celly looked at the card and realised it was the Dreeknian technology to keep bulky objects inside a thin small strap to be placed in pant pockets. Aiden tried to explain the technology to her but was stopped midway by CELLY. Soon he remembered that he received the box from a Dreeknian thus leading to the conclusion that the box is a Dreek technology and thus Celly knows about it. Celly at once realised that the man who had sent the heart must be a Dreeknian. The question now was why would an immortal guy like to die and how did a Dreeknian has crossed the boundaries of Dreek and survived normally among other human beings.

Aiden looked at them and said, "Sorry to interfere in your thoughts but I want you to know that you may think immortality is what everyone wants but as I have learnt from Karan's thoughts by touching his possessions, he was actually cursed with immortality and had lost his near and dear ones one by one while he went on living. The death of those people pierced his heart like a thousand needles and when it came to feelings and emotions, he was highly sensitive and would cry over the slightest sadness. Immortality is never a boon for mankind. I know it because I saw many of my loved ones die in front of me and got devastated, now just think the number of loved ones Karan would have lost in his long life time. The quantity must be so high that any normal human would have been calling the devil by now. Now I would like to ask you a question, that is why had Karan been cursed so dreadfully as I could see only those memories left within this body. The rest of it had been taken by him with him and into his heart where they are trapped with his consciousness. So, I want to know all about Karan. "

At first Celly hesitated to talk about Dreek to an outsider but seeing Aiden's determination, she saw there was no other option but to speak out about Karan. She began. "Before knowing about Karan you should know about the kings who ruled over this kingdom. The first dynasty was that of the Rashad. Five kings of that dynasty ruled for over three hundred years. They were one of the most stable dynasty to rule over a kingdom. During their period Dreek saw a steady and gradual growth in farming sector, but the fifth was the cause of Dreek's downfall as he was a dimwit and an irresponsible one. At that point, Rashad also saw the dynasty losing its territory to nearby countries thus the fourth king in his old age entrusted the kingdom to the Rashad dynasty's sixth commander-in-general who after the fourth King's demise killed the fifth of the Rashad and this marked the start of the Irfith dynasty.

"After ruling for one hundred and fifty years, the third king of the lineage was killed , as it is said 'Karma hits' as his forefather betrayed the kingdom and had killed the Rashad dynasty's king now the third of Irfith was betrayed and killed by his own army as he waged continuous war against various countries without any cause or reason. Even after losing many soldiers, he never stopped the war. His aim was to rule all over the world being the sole conqueror. The soldiers became frustrated and tired of the continuous wars. Thus they killed the king, and one of them became the next king as voted by the people of Dreek.

"Thus started the golden era of the Arhan lineage. The first king, Arhan, cared for his countrymen and looked after them well. This was the period when farms were developed and agriculture became stable and prosperous, there was a sudden economic growth and the country forwarded towards prosperity. The king could not last long and died due to some mysterious illness at the age of fifty. He had two sons; the older, Arhan-II and the younger Siharhan. According to the rules the older was declared the new king of Dreek but due to his love for younger brother he named his brother as the king of Dreek and he himself became the commander-in-chief of the army. Till date this fact is taught as an example of brotherhood to the children of Dreek.

Both the brothers worked hard for the development of the country and it was the period of large-scale infrastructural development. Poverty was more or less wiped out. They avoided war and tried to collaborate with as many countries as they could. Siharhan was married to Rimshi, the daughter of one of his minister, Singad. She helped the king in developing his kingdom.

Meanwhile Arhan-II who wanted to lead a normal life and no political marriage fell in love with a commoner girl named Freta and married her. The whole family was happy as well as the people of the kingdom but the kingdom of Hulstutus were jealous of the development in Dreek and wanted to take it over. The Hulstutus had always been supressed by the Dreeks as they were weaker than us, but seeing such young and inexperienced kings ruling over Dreek they thought it would be easy to defeat us and declared war against Dreek. Siharhan tried to compromise with the king of Hulstutu but he did not show any interest. Arhan-II became determined to fight the war.

But the flaw in the Arhan lineage was the development in army, the soldiers were given special privileges and rather than war strategy and tactics they were mainly taught to protect the people of the kingdom, They were more of a defensive army rather than offensive. This made them incompetent to fight in wars and so Dreek lost the war with Hulstutu. Arhan-II died fighting in the war and that was also one of the main cause of losing the war. Siharhan was heartbroken and asked for help from king Jungaad, the ruler of the Abhaari kingdom, to fight and defeat the kingdom of Hulstutu.

Siharhan did not only want to defeat Hulstutu; he also wanted to destroy the kingdom and wipe it off the face of the Earth. This is when the downfall of the golden era and the story of revenge started. After this, many wars were fought between Dreek and Hulstutu. Sometimes one lost sometimes the other but none of them were ready to stop warring.

Meanwhile, Arhan-II's son, Mararhan, grew up and started spending the treasury money extravagantly. Freta was depressed from the day her husband had died so she was not in a position to strict her son and as for Siharhan he couldn't be strict towards his beloved brother's son. Siharhan's son was not the exact opposite of his cousin but was much better than Mararhan. He would have chosen the same path as Mararhan but being kind-hearted he saw how much pain his country endured during the constant wars. He strongly wanted to end it.

Five years of war had continued.

Siharhan's son was now seventeen years old. He slipped into the enemy's kingdom in a bid to end the war. First, he lived as a commoner in the kingdom of Hulstutu; then he joined the army of Hulstutu and despite being highly skilled he shied away from fighting; leading everyone to believe he was a coward. Meanwhile, the Dreek kingdom was in chaos because of the war and the king and queen's concern for their lost child. They did not know where their son was and how he was.

Meanwhile, Hulstutu's kingdom was also in chaos. The constant war had created a shortage of manpower and the king ordered all able-bodied adults to join the army. This shortage of men decreased the security around the king's palace. Seeing this situation, Siharhan's son secretly entered the king's room by silently and skillfully killing his guards. He killed the king and then he rang the emergency bell in the king's room and ran away.

All the security men, guards, and workers ran towards the king's room. The news of his murder spread like fire and no one knew how it had happened, but was ure that it was the worlk of one of Dreek's men. At last, after five years of war, Dreek won Hulstutu. this news did not make the king and queen happy as they were still brooding over their missing son. Then, someone came to the king's court and informed that the person who had killed the king of Hulstutu was none other than Siharhan's son. Also, this son was none other than Karan or often referred to as Karanjioslaman in todays' world !

Chapter 14

KARANJIOSLAMAN

Hearing the story of Karan sent Clave, Sihira and Aiden into a state of astonishment. They were surprised by the outstanding bravery of a seventeen-year-old boy who did not just kill to avenge his uncle but also to end the long war that had resulted in so much pain and suffering for the citizens of both the countries. The three of them were eager to hear more about King Karan. Noticing their innocence, Celly's face beamed up a smile but she concealed it before anyone could notice and realised that she could trust them but it was too late to keep continuing as it was already night so she told them to eat some food and take rest. She promised them that she would narrate the rest of the story the next day.

After dinner, they went to bed but were restless over the many questions flooding their minds. They wondered how such a brave prince had been cursed with immortality, what had happened of Mararhan and why was there no statue of the Arhan dynasty. When they entered Dreek, they had not seen a single one despite the fact that the dynasty was mainly responsible of the kingdom's peace and development and the main question was why did Celly referred to Karan as Karanjioslaman.

Aiden could take it no longer and rushed towards Celly's room. Clave and Sihira followed him, but the guards stopped them thinking they were trying to escape. Clave tried to explain them the truth, but the guards kept ordering them to return back to their rooms. Hearing the commotion, Celly woke up and despite being tired from the day's work stomped down the stairs and shouted angrily" what is going on there? Don't you know it's 2a.m. at night and it is the time to be in deep sleep."

The three of them pleaded with her to narrate the rest of the story as they were restless and could not sleep because of their curiosity and the most of it they want to learn the mystery behind the name 'Karanjioslaman'. Seeing their innocence Celly's anger faded away and a broad smile was about to appear which she stopped and decided to narrate the whole story to them that night itself. The four of them sat down and Celly ordered some coffee. After a sip she started narrating. "At Hultustu, Karan who now had the authority equal to the king, opened their King's treasury and helped the poor to improve their lives. He also compensated the families of those who had lost their loved ones in battle.

"In a little while, Karan normalised the situation in Hultustu. He now introduced a system known as democracy; people can choose their own ruler. The votings soon started. The guards started roaming from house to house collecting pieces of folded papers with the name of whom the people wanted to elect. No one was surprised that majority had voted For Karan but he refused them as he had to return to his own kingdom of Dreek. He recommended that the people elect Mararhan as their new king. No one questioned him on his decision as they knew he wished their wellbeing, thus everyone agreed. he promised them that their new king would be with them soon and would help them develop and overcome the war damages.

"He left Hultustu and reached Dreek. Everyone cheered and a huge celebration took place for the prince of Dreek while Mararhan was also welcomed with a grand celebration. Karan talked to Mararhan and made him realise his responsibilities. He declared the love affair between his father and a girl named Arhila from Hultustu. This love story had begun during the war when Siharhan was devising new strategies to kill the king of Hulstutu; One of them was to disguise himself as an injured Hulstutu soldier and enter the kingdom and then kill the king and he himself chose to be the volunteer for this.

"However, before he could complete his mission he was really injured and being disguised as a Hulstutu soldier was taken to their camp medic where he was treated by Arhila. When the soldiers of Hultustu searched for the spy, Arhila saved the king from being discovered. He promised Arhila that once the war ended, he would marry her and now his son had fulfilled his promise. So that night, two celebrations took place—one the marriage of Siharhan and Arhila, and the second; Karan being declared the next king of Dreek.

"The kingdom of Dreek again saw development as the clouds of war and its consequent misery were blown away by Karan. Everyone was happy except for one person and that was Rimshi. She saw how the king spent most of his time with the new queen and that even his own son was treating Arhila as his mother and ignoring his real mother. Rimshi soon understood that her marriage was just a political alliance while Arhila was the true love of the king. This might lead to her being ignored by Karan and treated badly by Arhila.

"She feared that her position would soon be jeopardised so she tried different ways to get closer to the king; dressing seductively, trying to comfort him but all in vain as he would not notice all these and would run back to Arhila. However, the king was truly depressed that Arhila could not bear any children. She had some genetic disorder that rendered her unable to bear a child. Due to this, she cried a lot during her lone times. Therefore, Siharhan and Karan did not leave her side fearing she might hurt herself.

"Arhila cared for Karan as her own son and the care provided by karan made her forget about her infertility. She was happy but Rimsha could not take it any longer. She confronted Karan and told her how she felt lonely and ignored when both, her husband and son were paying all their attention to some other woman. Karan being compassionate did not see any negativity in this statement and thought her mother is innocent and just craves for attention, so to calm her he told her that arhila is getting more attention due to her inability to bear a child and that trauma may affect her, so to keep her away from that mental state of depression they had to give her more time. but Rimsha's sense of insecurity had already changed into fear which is not an empty erasable statement.

"She thought up a plan. She went to meet Mararhan, now the king of Hultustu, and told him how Karan had sent him to rule over Hultustu, the kingdom that had killed his father, Arhan-II. She said that Karan had done it to humiliate him and also to get the throne of Dreek for himself. Therefore, Mararhan should get his revenge by killing Arhila that would depress both king Siharhan and prince Karan. Then he could take over the throne of Dreek and rule over both Dreek and Hultustu.

Mararhan grew angry listening to all this. He agreed to Rimsha and planned to kill, but not Arhila; instead, he planned to kill king Siharhan so that Karan would feel pain of losing his father, but he did not reveal his plan to Rimsha. Mararhan sent one of his most able assassins to a public ceremony where the king, Siharhan was addressing the public about the development of the kingdom. As the king loved to spend time with his subjects he always addressed the crowd without any guards, thus the assassin got the perfect opportunity and stabbed him. Some persons ran to hold the king, while some caught hold of the assassin. There was chaos everywhere. The king was taken to the palace, and vaidyas were called to treat him. Even Arhila tried to treat him but it was too late. The assailant's knife had pierced a vital spot near his heart.

On his death bed, the king told Arhila to send a message to Karan, who had venturing to different coutries to learn about different people before being a king. On receiving the news he rushed back to Dreek and seeing his father in the irreparable condition , he broke into tears and the people who had caught the assassin told Karan it was done at the behest of Mararhan. Karan was about to launch war against Hultustu when Arhila stopped him saying that Siharhan's last message was to stop him from starting any war as it would only result in death, pain and suffering of civilians of both the countries. Karan also remembered the previous war and why he had to stop it, but the anger inside him was burning and growing.

Karan gave up his intention and completed the ceremonial rites and cremation. After that, Karan went to Mararhan as he wanted to keep his father's word to not let anyone else suffer for his personal grudges but he also wanted to avenge his murder. As soon as he reached Hulstutu, Mararhan was informed of his arrival. Mararhan was shivering because he knew what his brother was capable of, but he knew he can't avoid the situation thus he mustered up his courage and went met him. In his heart he was blaming Rimsha and himself; Rimsha because it was her plan and Himself because even after knowing his brother's strength he hurt his family. Karan without wasting another moment challenged Mararhan to a one-on-one fight without any rules or restrictions, a fight to death. Mararhan had no choice but to accept it, and even if he doesn't he would be killed right there by the beast standing right in front of him. So either way he dies thus he chose to die fighting. After a long and tiring duel, Karan felled him and twisted his neck.

Karan should have been happy after taking his revenge but he sat down and cried over his brother' dead body. He carried his body in his arms and went to his palace where he went to Freta's and placed it in front of her. She was speechless; even her eyes did not blink; she just stared into blank space. It was too much to bear as she lost both; her husband during the war and now her son. Karan left the body there and went away.

After a while, guards and other helpers came and realised that Mararhan's mother had succumbed to a heart attack, her last words as heard by the guards were "You will be cursed of seeing your own death again and again." They carried both the bodies to Dreek for the final rites. Karan reached his palace with his injuries and sat on the throne, bleeding and half conscious. Rimsha came running towards him and called for the medics. Karan looked at her with tears in his edyes and told Rimsha that Mararhan had told him the truth before he died.

Rimsha upon hearing this broke into tears and explained how she just wanted to harm Arhila and not his father. Karan did not say anything but declared that Hultustu would be merged with Dreek and both the nations will have the common name of Dreek. He would be the ruler of the combined nation. He told his ministers to announce this news all over the nations. Even if people were sad after losing Siharhan, they were happy to have Karan as their new king. On the other hand, the citizens of Hultustu were happy on being united with Dreek and Karan being their ruler, this way there won't be any war between the two nations anymore. Karan on the other hand decided not to harm his mother as he could not afford to lose any more of his family. From now on he decided to pay attention to Arhila and Rimsha equally.

Many a times Karan also tried to unite both of them but they were not ready to forget past enmity and jealousy and sink their differences. Rimsha was angry because of her fear and Arhila was angry as she considered Rimsha responsible for Siharhan's death, she is the reason for whom she lost her love of her life. Karan spent as much time as he could with both of them along with ruling over two nations.

It was quite difficult for Karan to juggle his responsibilities, and that too spending time with them together was impossible as they both hated each other to their cores. So, he decided to build another palace for Arhila. He would then be able spend half a month with Arhila and the other half with Rimsha, leaving him free to concentrate on national issues. He started the building of the palace. It was a grand project and had already taken eight years and thirty thousand workers to work on it. It was estimated that it could take more than twenty years more.

The workers, seeing the king's worry worked day and night to complete it as soon as possible. Rimsha's jealousy increased as Arhila's palace was even grander than her own. The citizen considered it a wonder of the era. Rimsha wanted it for herself but she could not tell Karan as she had already been accused of

Siharhan's death and felt that Karan would no longer recognise her as his mother if he came to know of her jealousy.

She remained silent, but when the half-month cycle started, Rimisha noticed how Karan spent the fifteen days with her by spending most of his time checking out national issues while with Arhila he spent his time happily with her without interfering in the national affairs. It was as if he was hating to stay with her birth mother and loving to stay with her step mother.

Meanwhile, the workers who had worked tirelessly to build the palace were named as Slamans which in the Dreek language meant 'master artisans' They were paid and rewarded handsomely. The Slamans were great followers of Arhila as she was kind and polite to everyone. This popularity of Arhila further ignited the fuel of jealousy inside Rimsha. One night she went to Arhila's palace and pleaded with her to go away as she was interfering in her family. She was the reason why Karan was ignoring his actual mother and she was the actual reason she lost her husband.

Rimsha broke into tears as she did not want to lose her son as well. Arhila realised how she had become a thorn in the side for their family. After Rimsha left, Arhila left the palace that night and since then there has been no news about her. Karan conducted many searches but it seemed Arhila was keeping an eye on Karan's movements, and shifted every time he reached anywhere near her.

Karan was depressed seeing he could not save any of his father's loved ones. After Arhila disappeared, Rimsha tried many times to make Karan smile but it was as if Karan had forgotten the meaning of happiness. He just worked as a labourer for the betterment of the country. He was married to the beautiful princess of Abhira, Lilith. She was famed to be the most beautiful lady of that era but Karan and Lilith were not passionate with each other as Karan had forgotten the meaning of emotions. Lilith was frustrated with Karan's behaviour and started having extra marital affairs.

Soon Karan learned about Lilith's extramarital affairs and he banished Lilith from Dreek without a second thought. During these tough times the only one who made him smile was an unknown girl yet a commoner. Lilith was humiliated and was labelled as a treacherous woman by the whole nation. She unable to handle this humiliation went to meet Rimsha after knowing about the bad relations between her and Karan. Lilith wanted to humiliate Karan to the maximum, because there was a time when people lined up only to get a glance of her but now due to Karan people threw hateful looks at her glance. Rimsha now had become a devotee of the devil, Halsifer. Rimsha's fear and jealousy had taken over her good parts and the last pint of love she had for her son had been lost; she only wanted to live for herself and as she had achieved all that had she ever desired, she just wanted one thing—immortality.

For that, she started worshipping the devil and as for the devil we know that he always wants something in return for a favour. Being a great devotee of Halsifer, she made a deal with him that Lilith's remaining year of her life will be added to hers. Lilith accepted it but said that before dying she wanted to see Karan's destruction. Thus both of them devised a plan to humiliate him. Rimsha had made some of the security men highly loyal to herself by giving them double the payment they used to get. She told them the plan and ordered them to do accordingly.

The next day, the Dreeknians were instigated by those guards to protest in front of Karan's palace. When Karan came out and saw them, he realised what had happened. Rimshi's guards had killed thirty the thousand Slamans and deliberately allowed themselves to be caught by the Dreeknians. During questioning they said that they had been sent by the king to kill the Slamans to ensure they wouldn't build a similar palace in the future for anyone else. Karan did not have anything to prove his innocence thus with a gloomy expression he walked down the palace stairs to the people. Many among them have lost their family members meanwhile the others had gathered to support them. They beat Karan and those guards to death. After their king's death there was no kingly candidate to be the next ruler, neither Karan had any children, thus a female ruler stood up to the responsibility and started ruling over them. She was none other than Rimsha. She started exploiting the resources as she had extra life; the remaining life of Lilith. She did everything extravagantly.

The Dreeknians were leading a truly miserable life of pain and suffering. The whole nation was poverty stricken. Among all these the only one who could have rescued the Dreeknians is the higher lord, and the miracle did happen; the Supreme landed in their midst. He took pity on them and blessed them with the intelligence, more than normal human brains.

The Dreeknians after gaining back their independance believed that outer interference was the main cause of their downfall because only after the interference of Arhila, a woman from another kingdom that the Arhan clan began declining. They made a machine to shield themselves from the outside world. It was a kind of radiation with little mind numbing elements inside it that when detects a brain leaving, it enters the mind and destroys the memories about Dreek, Anyone who ventured beyond it would go insane so that Dreek's secret would never be revealed.

Hearing about the massacre of the Slamans, the Supreme realised that it was a easy death for such a heinous crime thus he revived Karan and cursed him with immortality; he would be reborn after eighty years from different parents with different identities but retaining all the memories of his previous lives. This will ensure he remembered the pain and suffering for ever. He was also cursed with the emotions of all the thirty thousand Slamans so the pain he would feel would be thirty thousand times stronger than normal. Thus, the name 'Karanjioslaman': Karan for the king's name, Jio as in hindi meaning live and Slaman as in dreek meaning master Artisans. The name depicted the slamans living in Karan."

Chapter 15
MISSION

"After this curse, it was still not the end as we told the Supreme that Rimsha was the one the who played a dirty game by instigating Mararhan and now she had been given extra life, and as for Arhila the supreme denied any punishment for her as love is not a crime. The Supreme could not cancel the boon given by the Devil, but added diseases, pain and suffering to the extra life that Rimsha had gained. Till today, we did not know anything about Karan. The only thing we knew at Rimsha's death was that she was the one behind the death of those Slamans.

"However, only a few of us could know about it. Many people hated her even earlier and did not come when she died. We told everyone the story Rimsha had told us—how she was the one who had got the Slamans killed and that Karan was innocent. Some believed us while others did not. The ones who believed us became anti-nationalists and the ones who did not became nationalists. As they had a majority, they live openly while we the minority have to do our work in secret.

"We are still looking for evidence to prove Karan's innocence but could not. According to Karan's curse, the place where he dies is where he will be reborn, thus if Karan dies in Dreek he borns in Dreek but to different parents. The time he was revived he left Dreek as he felt guilty for the death of those slamans. This is the reason you were sentenced to death by the court as it is nationalist. They want to make you suffer for killing those, Slamans So they planned to kill you again and again to give you unending suffering, but luckily they did not realise that you are not Karan. So now tell me what do you think of Karan."

The three were speechless. They thought they had heard a fairy tale or a historical fiction, it was hard for them to believe that such incident actually took place. For some moments, they were not able to speak, even Aiden, not having any feelings or emotions played along with the other two and but could no longer take in the silence and spoke up. "Listen, I have this incredible power to know people's thoughts by physical contact with them but I don't have any control over it and don't even know how to use it. If you can teach me to master it, it may be of some use to you on your mission."

Celly looked at him doubtfully and said, "I never mentioned that power being used in the mission. It can be of use to you on your mission." Celly came towards him with her gun pointing at him. Aiden realised it would be better to tell the truth. "Everywhere there's something that brings out a surge of emotions in humans. The same also happens in me but the difference is other people have their hearts for the uniform distribution of those emotions and thus being controllable but in me there is no medium for these surging emotions to flow in me and thus they suddenly rise and demise and for that short period of time I became able to use the power.

"The first time it happened was when Sihira was involved in the accident and I saw her on the road; the second was when the driver was taking me to Lihamantos to find my parents and he was not telling me anything; the third was when Sihira was telling me her love story with Karan and the fourth is now after seeing you. I don't know why but it is as if I know you already.

"It may be because of direct contact with a person or not. Whenever I get a surge of emotions, I just enter their thoughts without even knowing it and get a glimpse of their memories. Please believe me that I don't have any control over this power but I do know for sure that my emotions can only activate this power and for that I need a heart, because that's the only thing missing in my body. As soon as I get the heart, I can find the source of the shield that is creating an energy barrier around Dreek."

Celly was shocked as to how Aiden had deduced out their mission and she realised that their mission was no longer a secret for them, now she truly believed that Aiden can read minds. She knew that they don't have to keep their mission a secret anymore so she spoke up, "The barrier that has been protecting us from ages and had been a blessing, but has also become a curse as we have no contact with the outer world. We are bored with our life inside the barrier with all this developed technology. We want to be free, with or without technologies, freedom is greater than any development and that both nationalists and anti-nationalists used to be on equal terms on this matter. However, from last some decades the nationalists no longer believe us as they have been brainwashed by the priests that we are the followers of the devil.

"They have been influenced to believe that anyone who tries to defy the Supreme will be destroyed and that the protective layer is the sacred sign of the blessing the Supreme has bestowed upon us. Therefore, we should not break it. They have brainwashed the people to such extent that people had forgotten what the ssupreme actually said; if we ever broke the barrier then these technological advancements would disappear and we could forget about the

Supreme and remember only the events till the death of our king- Karan. These were the facts told by the supreme which are exact opposite of what the priests say. The priests had modified the facts known by our forefathers and told it to brainwash the dreeknians. The supreme himself gave us a choice of living like normal humans, having our freedom or having everything and living as prisoners.

"The priests modified it and thus the nationalists no more want to break the barrier or interact with the outside world. I want to break the barrier but till now didn't have the resources but with you present now we can find the source and break it and prove Karan's innocence." Aiden agreed without any second thoughtt6. First, they needed to plant a heart in Aiden's body to give a medium for emotions to flow in his body.

That would help Aiden use the power. They could not plant Karan's heart as it could activate Karan's soul and harm Aiden. Besides, they were not sure if Karan would help so they tried to plant other hearts they had been preserving but every time they planted one Aiden would not wake up until they removed it and placed the artificial one he was living with. Aiden said that after every transplant he heard everything going around him but however hard he tried he could not move his body or wake up. Then they realised there was only way and that was to plant Karan's heart in that body as other hearts were not compatible. They were not sure of the result but they were ready to take the risk.

The procedures began and Aiden was given an anaesthetic. Aiden started losing consciousness. He talked to Celly before falling asleep.

"So, tell me who is the Supreme?"

"He is the son of the Almighty with similar power and rumoured to be next ruler of the whole multiverse after the Almighty."

"Multiverse?"

"Yes, there is not only one universe; rather there are many Universes. We don't definitely know how many."

"So it means I am from another world and was transferred to this world by Lucifer?"

"Lucifer?"

"Yes, the Devil of our world, like the Devil of your world, Halsifer; Lucifer is also cunning and shrewd."

"Ah! These devils are the root of every problem."

"Or the Supreme, we never knew about these creatures. Just think why did the Supreme suddenly emerge to help you all, isn't it......?"

Before he could complete, he lapsed into unconsciousness. The operation was complete and now they just had to wait for Aiden or Karan to wake up. Celly was thinking about the things Aiden had told her before the operation but the tension of who will be in the body that wakes was building up within her. After some hours, the body woke up. He looked around for a moment and heard someone calling him. "Aiden, Aiden, are you still Aiden?"

He looked in the direction of the voice and recognised it as Sihira's. He replied still in trance mode, "Yes, I am still Aiden" and continued, "Now I feel complete and happy too." He grafdually gained his whole consciousness. This time with more energy, he jumped down from the bed and started cheering.

Everyone was happy that Aiden was still alive. Most of all, Sihira was the happiest because she had fallen in love with Aiden, her obsession with Karan was long gone but her insanity was still clinging to her. This time they became sure that Karan won't wake up and thus they got their chance to complete the mission because Karan staying dormant would be an asset for them.

Aiden started concentrating on one person to see whether he can enter their mind and read their thoughts. He came to know through the dreek technology that all living and non-living creatures are connected by cosmic invisible threads. The Dreeks call it INR(Inter Norton Radiation) which means the internal security radiations that keep everyone and everything in this universe connected and secured. Thus, it becomes easy to prove the butterfly effect that is a small change in one state of a linear system can result in large differences in a later state. Aiden thought that by those threads he could easily use his powers as directly or indirectly he is connected to everyone. The trick was to learn how to picturise a person and concentrate on the energy thread that connected him with that person. He could then read his thought by holding on to that thread.

After much trial and error, he realised he saw the thoughts in a human brain like a movie projection in a theatre and if that was the case, he could re-form their thoughts and replace it with different ones. In this way he could lead them to believe that Karan was innocent and that the massacre was the handiwork of queen Rimshi, what he has to do is that once he enters their mind he has to connect their brain and his and only picturise the incidents that he wants to place it inside due to which these new thoughts will override the olden chosen memories. He had to be careful to do it in such a way that their other thoughts remain intact and any of his other thoughts don't get included in their minds.

Aiden first rehearsed the story he would put in people's minds regarding the Queen's death and her involvement in the massacre, he kept picturising it again and again. He increased his focus power so that any other thoughts won't cross his mind while replacing the thoughts about Karan. After many days of training it over and over in his mind, he realised that if he tried to do individually, it would a long time. He needed to perform the task collectively and change everyone's mind at one go. This too he had to practice for many days.

After the completion of his training and practice, Aiden laid out the step-by-step plan. It was put into operation and it seemed quite easy. First, Aiden re-formed the people's minds by pressing and imposing the picturised thought of Karan being innocent in them. After this worked successfully, they started searching for the sources of the barrier. It was a tiresome job as they had to penetrate many minds to get the smallest of clues.

He could have re-formed their minds into giving out the secret but anything related to the Supreme was strictly forbidden. As they didn't know the consequences of challenging a higher form. Besides, the priests' allegations were still deeply instilled in the minds of the people and the fact that if they defied the Supreme, they would be destroyed.

Realising this hurdle, it was decided that Celly and others and Aiden would identify people whose thoughts would be checked by Aiden, as checking so many minds at a time was a tiresome job and Aiden took a great toll on his mind due to which he suffered severe headaches. Celly and her workers made various categories but Aiden thought of trying something on his own. He searched the priests' minds and discovered the truth about the sources and where they had been hidden.

Aiden told Celly about it. She asked how he knew that the priests were the actual keepers of the secrets. Aiden told her his theory. "See, during your period there was no particular section of priests and anyone who worshipped a god, worshipped on their own and not through a priest. Why had the priests risen suddenly after the Supreme's visit? Because those were the people who knew the secret of the shield thus The locals believed that the priests were blessed by the Supreme actually referring to the secrets they were told, unknown to the others.

"On entering their minds, I saw that the ancestors of the priests built the machines that were kept in the four directions around Dreek and were activated and strengthened using the Supreme's power. The priests promised never to leak the secret and thus they abandoned the path of science and technology and became priests so no one would doubt them.

Celly advised them that now that they know the location of those machines they can easily pull it out and destroy it, but Aiden shook his head and said that the main problem was that the machines were buried deep in the ground outside the boundaries of Dreek. Someone has to cross the boundary to destroy them.

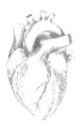

Chapter 16

MIND FIGHT

Everyone was tired running errands and making plans. Aiden was the most tired one with persistent headaches. They had their food and as they lay in bed they fell into deep sleep. Aiden woke up but not in the physical world rather in his own mind, at first he thought it may be some side effects due to the overuse of his powers but then he saw a throne in front of him with Karan sitting on it. The two looked at each other silently for some moments and Karan broke the silence.

"So, you proved my innocence."

"You must be at ease now, why don't you take over your body?"

"As if I could do that! Just go on and complete your tasks."

"Oh! Come on, you can take over this body easily."

"Let's just ignore that fact for now and let me know how do you plan to complete the mission?"

"I don't know, we need some plan."

"You are the plan."

"What! What do you mean?"

"Figure it out yourselves and, yes, I can easily take back my body. I just saw your determination to live."

"You think I am weak?"

"Nah; you are not that weak, rather iam that strong."

They looked at each other for some moments and started fighting each other. After a long and tiring fight they sat down and this time Aiden set the conversation rolling.

"So, why were you sitting on a throne?"

"That's how you picturise me in your mind, don't you?"

"So, it all depends on one's thoughts."

"See, you are strong enough to prevent Karan from taking over that body."

Saying this, he faded away. Aiden woke up without any headaches, looked around, and smiled. He went to Celly's room, she was sleeping peacefully in her trousers. When he saw her, he felt for a moment that Celly must be the cutest girl he had ever seen. He realised that she showed her tough and rude side to the world but behind the curtains, she was just a cute and shy girl. As soon as Celly was about to change her side, a little peek through her eyes noticed Aiden outside her open door peeking at her, in her haste to get some sleep at night she had forgotten to lock the door, she closed the door, changed her trousers, splashed some water on her face, and came out.

Now the smile on Aiden's face disappeared, he realised that now he has to deal with the rude one and the cute girl he enjoyed watching a moment ago is gone. He told her that he had worked out a plan to destroy the source of the barrier. He said that he is the one who should do it as he was neither a Dreeknian nor of the outer nations. He has survived in both places and moreover he, Aiden is not even from this world. He suggested that the curse might not even work on him. Celly was speechless. She told him to reconsider.

Aiden was confused and asked, "Hey! What do you mean by reconsider, this is the only way, this is the only plan. Look at the Dreeknians, they are confused after their thoughts were replaced. They are imagining why did the supreme punish karan even if he was innocent. So whatever we have to do we have to do it as soon as possible as once the barrier removes they will forget all about the supreme, the developments and the technologies and with only one thought that karan was innocent and everything was done by his mother, they can lead their life peacefully with Karan ruling them happily ever after." Celly turned to him and asked him why he thought it was a foolproof plan and what guarantee did he have that harm would not befall him when he crossed the barrier.

Aiden told her about his encounter with Karan to which Celly replied, "He himself said that due to your strong mental strength to survive, he was unable to take over his body? So, it means he may be tricking you into insanity so that after that he can easily take over his body again." Aiden replied, "Why do you care so much about losing me and, secondly, I saw the truth in his eyes; he just wants to be freed from immortality. So, Let's try this."

Celly nodded and went back into her room. Aiden shouted behind her, "You didn't answer my first question and, yes, I forgot to say another thing; you look cute when you are sleepy in your pyjamas." Saying this, he went away. Celly felt her heart skip a beat, her cheeks turned red and she started having lewd thoughts. Not giving it a second thought, she went off to sleep.

The next morning, they began setting the plan in motion. One of them asked 'what if a man from inside of the barrier tried to dig till he reached the source outside of the barrier , that is through underground. Aiden replied that whether it was digging or flying in the sky, the barrier would still destroy one's mind who crossed the boundary. Because the barrier has limited by distance and radius but by height and depth it's unlimited. He said them not to worry as it would be easy for him to destroy the source as he knew their exact location.

If anybody else was to go, then drawing a perfect map posed a challenge. A rope was tied around Aiden's waist to pull him back if he felt any adverse effect when crossing the boundary. He would signal by tugging the rope and the people inside the barrier would immediately pull him back.

Aiden looked at Celly but she turned away. He walked to her and spoke, "So this rope idea was yours? I see how desperate you are to save me. Don't worry, nothing will happen to me and if you think something will happen and you may not see me again, it's better you tell me now if you have anything to say." Celly kept quiet but she put a collar microphone on him and told him he could connect with her through it.

If anything happened, they will pull the rope swiftly. As Aiden advanced towards the boundary, his heart began pounding. He placed one of his feet outside the barrier. Sihira unknown of all these came walking from a distance unaware of the situation She ran towards him shouting he couldn't leave them behind as they promised to leave the country together. Some people tried to restrain her but it was in vain, she aggressively pushed through to reach him. Clave also tried chasing her but was caught by one of Celly's men.

Aiden had already passed out of the border. He could not hear anything. Sihira was running faster now, suddenly she tripped near the boundary and fell outside of it. Aiden saw Sihira to his side on the ground. His eyes opened wide; he could not speak for a moment but soon mustered up courage, ran to her, carried her in his arms and ran back into Dreek crying for help. Clave had turned white out of fear and his mind went blank. Aiden saw this situation of his but tried to focus on sihira for now.

Celly came running with the paramedics. They checked her. She was alive but they were not sure if she would be alright or would have gone insane by the time she gains consciousness. Aiden sighed and walked out again. Sihira was taken to the hospital. Aiden realised he had returned fit and fine so they should cut the rope but Celly refused to it even though Aiden kept insisting. She remained adamant. They therefore had no choice but to send Aiden with the rope tied to his waist. Aiden smiled at her concern and innocence and walked with the rope even after knowing that it would slow him down. After he reached the desired spot outside the boundary , he dug a shallow hole and planted an explosive just a little above the source machine.

He did so on the other three sides too. After gaining a safe distance from those he switched the trigger and the explosives went off with four sharp blasts. He suddenly tried to shout through the microphone for help but the communication device did not work across the barrier thus the only thing the people inside the barrier could hear were distorted voices. Aiden pulled at the rope. The people inside started drawing him in as fast as they could but suddenly they started to feel heavy and the pulling in slowed down. Eventually, the end of the rope returned without Aiden.

Celly knelt and started crying and shouted to Aiden through her microphone. "Aiden, please return, please don't die on me. I don't want to lose you, please return." While she was crying and shouting, the barrier began collapsing, and she heard a voice on her device, "You won't lose me, and now that you have said it, You won't ever be losing me." She looked up and saw Aiden standing in front of her with a broad and teasing smile on his face. After some staring, she stood up and slapped him.

The barrier was falling. The people were forgetting all about the Supreme, the technologies were fading away. They fell asleep along with Celly. When the people of Dreek woke up, they saw Karan sitting in front of them. They bowed to their king but they did not realise it was Aiden who is in Karan's body. He stood up and declared,

"Your king is back, the true culprit as you all know, my mother Rimsha is long dead. From now on I will work for the development of this nation." The only doubt the people had was how did karan survived for hundreds of years without aging a day. This was also answered by Aiden, "I by the blessings of God has been reincarnated on this land to bring properity to my land and my people." He looked at them with confused looks if they would believe it or not. After some moment of silence the people started murmuring and discussing, and eventually accepted it to them karan is a kind and compassionate king who never lies to his public and above all he looked like Karan; what more proof do they need than this. After the crowd dispersed he took a sigh of relief and

walked to Celly and looked at her. She was confused and asked, "Why do I remember everything." Aiden smiled and explained that when he went to meet her the previous night, he had thought of a plan to copy her past memories and over lay it over her existing memories. "Thus, your original memories got wiped out and the copied memories stayed." Celly shockingly asked him "You can do that too?"

Aiden wrapped his hand around her waist pulled her near and replied, "I can do many more that you are still unaware of."

Celly hugged him, but she felt a sudden shock in her brain and a question just blurted out of her involuntarily:

"Are these your feelings or Karan's?"

"I really don't know, but I have this strong feeling of owning you and I don't care whose it is. I can only say that I love you, and these are my feelings."

Celly was not satisfied; she wondered if some day Karan's soul faded away and then Aiden's feeling for her would also fade away. She wanted to be sure. Aiden had nothing to reply to thi, so he just chose to remain silent. These situations were as new as to him as it was to celly.

Celly realised the conversation was not over so she continued,

"The common girl I spoke of in Karan's story the one who made him smile during his hard times is none other than me. I was reincarnated because the Supreme thought that when Karan returned to Dreek he might find me, his love, as taking away everyone and everything would be so cruel a punishment, but to tell you the truth, I have never loved Karan but just stayed with him because he was in a lot of pain and pressure and being our king he had forgotten happiness. All these years, I have never loved anyone. Now I feel for you, see I can say my true feelings. So now can you guarantee the same to me?" Aiden again chose to stay silent and avoided any eye contact with her. Celly realising the depth of the situation said, " promise me that you will identify your true feelings before it's too late."

Aiden promised to do something about it. Just then, Clave arrived with the unconscious Sihira in his arms. Aiden told Celly to take care of her while he talked privately with Clave. He asked him, "You love Sihira, right? You were the one who helped her escape from the mental asylum so that you could save her and she would fall in love with you but unfortunately before she could reach you she met with an accident. Then I happened to pass from there and saved her and unfortunately became her hero."

"As you have read my thoughts, you should also know that I have no intention of taking her away from you as she is happy with you and I don't want to spoil that happiness of hers."

"But I don't love her." Said Aiden

"What!"

"Have I ever said that I love her?"

"Yes...No, you always said you would protect her."

"Is it same as love?"

"No, but she would never love me."

"I think, You forgot I have the power to re-form people's minds. I will replace me with you in her mind."

"No, I don't want to deceive her."

"Me too...that's why I want her to live with you who is the one who actually loves her. I don't love her. Even if I marry her, I would only keep her with me, like an object, not as a wife. I could never give her the love she wants, do you want her to be deceived for the rest of her life?."

Clave thought for some moments trying to understand him and thus agreed to him. Aiden entered Sihira's mind and did as he had told Clave. After that, they waited for her to wake up to confirm she had not gone insane, she woke up seeing Clave near her and hugged him. Aiden and clave looked at each other and smiled as they understood that their task was accomplished. Celly assured Aiden that with the barrier gone any curse related to it had also vanished. All those who had become insane after leaving Dreek would now become normal.

Aiden went with Celly to Karan's palace to tell her something important. "I lost everything...my father, my mother, and the girl I loved on the previous planet, in my previous life. Now I have lost Sihira also. Even if my first love and my mother have survived that is if Lucifer has kept his part of the deal, it's a pity I am not with them." Celly smiled softly and replied, "It's all fate; everything is interconnected.

If Rimsha had not been here, neither Karan would be there and neither you. So, I let you embark on this amazing adventure and enable you to learn what life is and the importance of the Devil, even if I knew karan wouldn't disagree to help us I wanted to be present here to complete the mission so that you will be able to learn about the importance of life. I smiled over your innocence when you craved to hear Karan's story, and I never denied to it as Karan's story is a true inspiration of courage, bravery and valour. I also realised along the way that God and devil both should exist to keep a balance, bother good and evil should prevail for the existence of humans, thus My hatred for Halsifer had decreased drastically."

Aiden smiled at her and after some moments of staring into each other's eyes, he kissed her on her forehead and slowly advanced to her lips. After a warm and tender kiss on the lips he told her he really did not care how Karan felt. The truth is he loves her and the question is; is she willing to accept him, despite the fact that he lives in someone else body. Celly immediately agreed and said that she was thinking along the same lines but was hesitant to acknowledge it wondering what would happen if Karan re-entered his body. She also threatened Aiden that if he changed his feeling for her, she would beat him to death.

Aiden was happy to hear this. The smile from his face faded and with a serious look asked an important question. Was she willing to travel with him to another world? Celly nodded and said that she would follow him to the end of the universe. Aiden said he was not speaking metaphorically, he has some aims to achieve and also had doubts to clear, The Supreme could have hidden the sources at much better places. Why had he hidden at such an easy to find place? and why did he install such easily destructible sources? He wanted to find the truth behind The Supreme. Above all, he also wanted to see if his mother was fine or not.

Celly listened to all this and sighed that it might be impossible now as all the technologies were destroyed along with the barrier. Even if she could remember how to build an inter-dimensional transporter, she would not be able to do so as the necessary equipment had also disappeared with the technology. Therefore, Aiden's dream could not be fulfilled.

Aiden hugged her and whispered, "May be everything's not destroyed. You said the technologies inside Dreek were destroyed. What if there was something outside the barrier. Will it also be destroyed?"

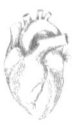

Chapter 17
CHOSEN LIFE

Celly looked at him surprised; she was unable to speak. She spoke with a shaky voice, "Did you hide anything without us knowing?" Seeing the tension, Aiden smiled weirdly and said that he had taken the dimensional teleporter unit out of the barrier and had hidden it in a safe place in the jungle. Celly's eyes opened wide. She asked again, "So you already knew that the curse of the barrier would not affect you?" At this, Aiden became speechless but on Celly's angry look he said, "The night before destroying the sources, after visiting your room I tried to do some experiments like going out of the barrier and taking some assets with me to check if they could exist outside the barrier. The machinery stopped working as soon as it was taken out, but I returned safely."

Celly was angry that Aiden had hidden the fact that crossing the barrier would not have hurt him. She had been crying unnecessarily like a fool. Aiden smiled and told her that that if she wouldn't have cried, he wouldn't have realised her love and would have married Sihira whom he never loved. It was not such a convincing answer but enough to calm her in the current situation.

Celly said, "Now, to the main topic. The Supreme always warned us that any technology of Dreek that they received from him should not be exposed to the people outside Dreek. If that happened, he would kill everyone. We don't know why he said this but no one had the courage to question the Supreme. Above all, he made our life better so we thought it better to just obey him."

Aiden said he had no other choice and now they just had to go to that place and check if the transporter was still there or not. Without wasting another minute they rushed to where Aiden had hidden the transporter and luckily found it still there. Sihira tried starting it but the machine was already dead. Aiden told her to repair it. Celly refused saying that she didn't know anything about science. Aiden pointed at a name etched on the lower wall of the machine. It said 'Wally Ackorstu.'

"You are Celly Ackorstu, right, which means he must be your relative or something."

"Yes, he was my father, but I won't repair it."

"Are you scared to repair it?"

"No, not scared, but...."

"Come on, say it, no one is going to judge you."

"Will you leave me once I build it?"

Aiden looked at her and laughed. He said that he won't be going alone and that she would be accompanying him on the journey as they had discussed. Celly smiled back and hugged him. They carried the transporter into the palace and Celly said that she would start working on it from tomorrow. They both went to sleep. Celly was still not confident enough thus she went into another room to think more about it.

Soon Aiden went into his domain of thoughts again where he met Karan and this time, Aiden started the conversation.

"So, you still don't want this body?"

"No, but you need me in it."

"Why?"

"Only because of me holding onto your memories did not let the barrier erase it. You have longer lifespan than others and that makes you stronger to use the power you have on a mass scale but when you include my immortality you can use that power on a much larger mass."

"Okay, thank you but Why would I need to use it on a larger mass?"

"You just used it on a large mass. 'reformed the memories of a whole country', who do you think gave you the power to do it? You never know the future but one thing is that two powerful souls make this body indestructible."

Aiden thought for some moments and asked.

"So, what do you want? Do you want to swap places with me whenever you want or do you want me to remain in this body?"

"I want neither...I just want that you ensure the development and security of Dreek as there are many precious resources in it as now with the shield gone, the other countries may find out about them and try to exploit them for themselves. Before they find out anything, you must find the resources and use them for the development of Dreek."

"Yeah, sure, I will take up the development of Dreek from tomorrow and, yes, another thing, I am not immortal. My soul has the added lives of the people who died due to the cursed tale, so I live longer than others."

"That's the reason the Devil couldn't destroy your soul, because he is the one who gave you the curse and thus he couldn't cancel it; he just wiped out your timeline of that world and sent you to this one."

"How come you know about my story and the theories you just related...?"

"They were your theories, I know. We both belong to this same body so our thoughts will overlap; you will know mine; I will know yours. Now wake up, its already morning, and Celly must be waiting for your instructions."

"But...."

"No buts, now go, if you have any other questions, come at night."

"Don't talk like that; it sounds weird, 'I will come at night, but to talk'. Wait, wait, before leaving, just tell me whether my feelings for Celly are mine or yours?"

"I always felt a barrier stopping me from loving Sihira or any other girl but I never knew Celly was the barrier. Can't you figure it out for yourself? You felt a surge of power every time you felt something strong emotionally whether it be anger, sadness, happiness or love and while talking with Celly you felt the same. So, think yourself."

"But...."

Before Aiden could complete his sentence, he woke up and realised Celly was knocking on the door. He rushed to open it. She came in stomping and searching for something. Aiden was confused.

"What are you searching for?"

"I heard you talking to someone."

"What, no; wait, yes."

"So, who was it? It must be Sihira. You have not re-formed her mind."

"Hey no, I was talking to Karan in my thoughts. I never realised the voice and words came out of the real body."

"So that's why I heard two voices."

"Yes, one was mine and the other was Karan's, both coming from this body. You know, I confirmed today that these are truly my feelings."

Celly looked embarrassed and apologised for doubting him. Aiden comforted her, hugged her, and said that it's common in love. "Once you start loving someone truly, you can't even imagine him/her with someone else and that's called jealousy, which is fairly common in a relationship. It shows how much you love your partner and want him/her all to yourself and that's possessiveness."

Celly hugged him tightly and pressed her head against his chest. She said, "I don't care to know the answer, if it's you or that Karan who loves me, I know that I love you and that what matters. So I now feel somewhat at ease. I love you, Aiden." Aiden's heart started beating faster, his temperature rose. He did not know if he was happy, excited, or nervous. He was speechless. Celly thought Aiden had not heard what she said and she ran away embarrassed to look him saying she would begin working on the transporter after breakfast.

Aiden nodded and was still in shock. He realised how cowardly he had been. He should be the one to propose to her but even after listening to her he could not reply. After breakfast, they went to the room where they had transferred the transporter to. They talked for some time. Aiden told her about his conversation with Karan. Celly replied that he had also felt the power surge during Sihira's accident.

Aiden remained silent, but suddenly realised something and spoke, "That's what Karan was trying to say. I felt the power surge whenever I felt a strong emotion regardless of whether it was sadness or love. In the case of Sihira, it was sadness for her condition and the curiosity of my dreams. With you it is pure love, and that's the difference."

Celly understood. She smiled shyly and began working on the machine while Aiden went out to work for the development of the nation. He first appointed some ministers, and then some security men to guard the nation. He ordered Clave to talk to his people in Milatintia and bring in guns and modern technologies, as the Dreek technology have gone back to hundreds of years and even now a simple technology like radio is also lost to them.

Clave's men came as directed. Karan's butler also came with his men, at first he was shocked but soon after hearing the whole story about Aiden's adventure and Karan's presence, he understood the whole situation and adapted to it. They brought many items with them. They taught people the various technologies that today's world was using. Cell phone, television, refrigerator, and many things of utility. Aiden kept on thinking the resources that Karan had mentioned. He had said they are present in Dreek. He started exploring the two palaces—that of the King and the one Karan had built for Arhila.

In the latter he found the treasury, crores of worth of golds and diamonds but this was just the trailer. He found a room, but the key was not available as the room had not been opened for ages. He broke the lock open and was surprised to see the room filled with antiques.

They were worth billions and trillions of money. Aiden closed the door and came out, called some of Clave's men and told them to guard the palace strictly. An education system was established. Now Aiden had the money for workers and materials for schools, colleges, and hospitals. His butler brought in workers, doctors and many other professionals and soon the infrastructural development was initiated.

One evening as Aiden was strolling around in the farms when his eyes suddenly caught a glimpse of some different liquids leaked out of a crack in the land. He realised what it might be but to be sure he touched and smelled it and realised that was the resource that Karan had talked about. Dreek is a mine of petroleum and other fuels. Karan was filled excitement as now Dreek's economy will skyrocket and development will be faster than ever, the butler was ordered to start drilling and place the machineries to extract the fuel in its raw form. Thus, an all-round development of Dreek was taking place.

Busy in so many varied tasks, Aiden had to neglect Celly quite a lot as he did not have much time to spend with her. Celly started feeling neglected and became angry. When she had some free time, she talked to people who had come from outside Dreek. She learnt about their culture, and lifestyle. She slowly started understanding humans.

She saw that many belonged to different caste, religion and region and despite these differences they worked together for the development of Dreek. Celly stood in the balcony and was wondering about the outside world when Aiden came and stood beside her. Celly still angry at him, ignored him. Aiden realised his mistake and apologised but Celly had no intention of relenting. He grabbed her hand and apologised.

He saw no other option and thus, knelt down on one knee and proposed to her by giving her the ring of Rashad, the first ruler of Dreek. "It's the symbol of true love and loyalty. How did you get it?" Celly asked him confused. Aiden did not know what it was worth, he just found it to be beautiful thus aquired it from the treasury he found at Arhila's palace, he pretended that he knows all about the ring.

"Yes, this ring of Rashad is the symbol of true love and loyalty. I, Aiden, the king of Dreek, give it to you and offer you the status , that the first king Of the Rashad dynasty offered to his love, that is the status of queen."

"Can you say it in simpler terms?"

"Celly, will you marry me?"

"Yes, I will."

And thus being the shortest proposal in human history ,Celly advanced her hand. Aiden slipped the ring on to her finger and stood up. They hugged each other and Aiden called in his ministers and told them to declare that he and Celly are going to get married. This is what Aiden had always dreamed of, a life with both happiness and sadness, a true love and his own little family. As soon as the news spread, people rushed to the palace and waited eagerly for the king and the would be queen to come out and announce it themselves. Aiden and Celly holding each others hand came on to the balcony and looked down at the eager faces waiting for their declaration. Aiden declared, "From now on, I, Aide...I mean I, Karan, the King of Dreek, pronounce Celly to be my future wife and the queen of Dreek." Everyone cheered happily and Celly hugged Aiden.

The whole nation was decorated with flowers and lights; the whole atmosphere was filled with cheerful and happy sounds. The marriage was scheduled for three days later. All the preparations were completed by then, but the confusion was how to maary; in Dreeknian's style of culture oraccording to the world beyond Dreek. Aiden proposed that they should marry twice following different styles both time. Celly happily agreed to it. Rhus here in Dreek It was a Dreek-style marriage. The groom and bride gave gifts to each other and asked the visitors for their approval of their marriage. Once everyone did so they would ask each if they would love and care for each other till death. After both had accepted, they would exchange rings and hug each other thus completing the marriage.

Aiden told Celly to look at sky that was soon filled with the light and sound thousands of crackers bursting in the night sky. Celly could not hide her happiness after seeing the beautiful sight in front of her and jumped in excitement.

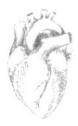

Chapter 18
THE LOOP

Celly looked around, grabbed his hand, pulled him towards herself, and whispered something in his ears. Aiden's eyes opened wide and he hoisted her above and put her down when the priest announced the completion of the marriage. Celly grabbed his hands and both of them ran towards the palace. Clave and Sihira realised that something was fishy so they followed them, but the audience thought it was the excitement of the newly married. Aiden and Celly were so excited that they did not realise they were being followed.

They reached the room where Celly had been working. She opened the door and showed him the dimensional transporter. So, this was the gift Celly was talking about. She had repaired the dimensional transporter and this was the greatest gift for Aiden as he longed to see his mother and his first love. They hugged each other in excitement but Celly warned him that the machine had never been used earlier so it was not a guaranteed to give the best of results.

This was the happy moment that will not be celebrated by the whole nation but only by the both of them. While they were discussing about the machine, Clave and Sihira started talking from behind. Clave told, "When were you planning to tell us about this?" Aiden and Celly were taken by surprise. Clave said that they had realised a long ago that there was something fishy going on between the two of them as since the last some days they have been spending way too much time in private and talked in gesture while in public, thus they had followed them and overheard their conversation. "So, you were planning inter-dimensional travel to meet your mother and you didn't care telling us. Do you feel we would have stopped you? do you not consider us your friends anymore?"

Aiden looked at him expressionless and told him, "We will be using this machine tomorrow so if you both also want to travel with us, you are welcome." Aiden and Celly left the room and went towards what was now their common room. Clave and Sihira followed. Seeing this, Aiden also shouted, "Not now, you fool, follow us tomorrow when we use the machine." Both of them fled and Aiden and Celly had a passionate first night.

The next morning, they had their food and waited for Sihira and Clave. When they came, Celly started the machine. She set the location but remembered that they did not know the location of the Earth they were supposed to land on. Aiden told her that during his last conversation with Karan he had learnt that they had to land on Earth-7.

Celly set the location and told Aiden that when he entered the machine, he has to press the button that would disintegrate his body to an atomic level. The second step would be that the disintegrated atoms, travelling faster than light, will integrate on the desired location.

Aiden had a question. He wanted to know if there was no similar machine on that planet, then who will integrate the atoms to re-form to their original self. Celly explained, "In a type-1 civilisation, two machines are needed—one from where you disintegrate and the other where you integrate. This dimensional transporter is a type-2 civilisation-made. Thus, the glue rays will travel with the disintegrated atoms and they will retain the memory to re-form your body into its original shape once they reach the desired location without any second machine."

Both of them entered the machine and told Clave and Sihira not to change any setting and just to press the blue button after after they teleport, as that machine can teleport only two at a time. Aiden and Celly were transported but there was a problem in the glue ray memory because of a wire malfunction. Consequently, during the alignment of their atoms, it had loosened due to which Celly's body was integrated wrongly that in turn killed her.

Meanwhile Aiden after integration also was not formed properly and his death led to his birth again on the Earth-7. When he woke up, he saw he was in a school, he looked at himself in the mirror and was shocked to see his old self in a younger version. The place where he woke up was his own school where he had studied. He saw his school friends, Jacob and Albin. He thought he was dreaming. He pinched, slapped, and punched himself but he only felt pain. He realised he was truly in his world and thus concluded that the Karan's life he was living was a dream. The first thing he asked his friends, Jacob and Albin was whether people were still dying

Mysteriously. His friends answered positively.

Aiden told them of the book, the cursed tale. He rushed to the police station with them and told the police officer everything but the police did not believe him and put them behind bars.

Aiden realised he should not have told them the truth; rather he would have done the same he had done in his dream that was publishing in the book and then would have acted as if he wanted to kill humans for which Jacob would hate him and then kill him. This would have ended the curse. When Jacob and Albin pleaded with him to stop all that, Aiden very carelessly told them to die. Jacob, angry that he had lost his father, took a police gun and shot him dead.

Aiden again fell into a pit of darkness and woke up but this time in Karan's body. The events he had experienced earlier in Karan's body that he thought to be a dream took place again. Before taking off in the dimensional transporter, Aiden told Celly to recheck the wires. Celly did so and realised that there was a small wiring problem in the integration system glue. She wondered how Aiden had suspected it.

Aiden silently grabbed her and entered the machine and reached Earth-7 again. This time because of the locator's mistake they were integrated on a railway track and a train passed over them. Celly and Aiden died again and again Aiden was reborn. This time he woke up to find himself in Sivara, as a young man. His mother called him for food. He was confused over what was going on but seeing his mother alive, he became emotional and hugged her. His mother was confused but hugged her back. He checked the date and realised it was the day of her death. He thought of changing the future so he didn't go to school that day.

However, his friends came to his home searching for him. As soon as Reinese and Suhasha arrived, Aiden got a call from his workplace to come ASAP but Aiden put them off. Reinese and Suhasha started making the report so they asked Aiden's mother questions. It was time to narrate the tale for the report.

Aiden remembered how the curse kills thus he stopped her from narrating it and narrated the whole story to them himself. After some days, the police came to their house asking about the mysterious deaths of Reinese and Suhasha. Aiden realised they must have narrated the story to someone and that killed them. The police interrogated Aiden and his mother separately. While doing so, Aiden's mother related the story that Aiden had told Reinese and Suhasha for their report. The next day she died.

Aiden was frustrated and shouted to kill him saying that Reinese and Suhasha were dead and only a close one with enough hatred in his/her heart could kill him. So he went to Yelena and after sweet talking her during days of friendship, he proposed to her and then acted that he wanted to kill most of the people leaving only a few to create a better world.

Yelena did not have the courage to kill him but Jennifer persuaded her to kill him by giving her various reasons. She told her if she didn't kill him, then he would kill many people, wiping out much of the civilization. Jennifer convinced her to kill him as she loved Yelena and believed that Aiden had taken her away from her. At last Yelena relented, and killed him.

Aiden again fell into a dark pit and woke up in Karan's body. He started shouting. This time also the he lived Karan's life in the same way as the previous one and after reaching the part of life where he used the transporter he told told Celly before teleporting to place the locator correctly as they need to land at the desired place. Celly was impressed by Aiden's intelligence and praised him. He whispered that experience always works. Again, they landed on Earth-7. This time they landed on a rooftop as set by Celly and when they reached there, Celly fell off the roof and died again. The same happened to Aiden and this time he woke up as a child with his father by his side.

He just goes on doing the things he had done in his previous life, dies, and again wakes up as Karan. He reaches the dimensional Transporter again. He realises he is trapped in an infinite loop and realised that neither can the things he had done in the past can be changed nor can the future be changed; it was all pre-destined. However hard he tried, and in whatever manner, he always lost everyone. Even changing his methods did not have any different result. He grabbed Celly's hands before she could activate the teleporter and told her there was no way he could spend time with his family any more. He realised that he has to accept the new reality and his new life. He narrated the entire story to her and broke into tears.

Celly patted him on his back and tried to console him. She said, "Parents take care of their children till adulthood. Then they get them married, after which they soon leave their parents. The parents die either of old age or other circumstances. So just think like this that your parents got you married and you have your own family now. Your present circumstances do not allow you to spend time with them. The Devil had told you that he had wiped out your existence, so when you land on that planet a new timeline of yours appears, again reviving the curse and the loop continues. So just accept that and try to live with us. Living with Evelyn and Yelena was your past meanwhile living with us is your present and future. You can't leave your present just to live in the past. That's what life is all about 'remember your past but try to move on to your future.'"

Aiden looked at her with tear-filled eyes and hugged her tightly. Celly patted his head and told him to sleep as he must be tired.

He placed his head on her lap and fell asleep immediately. She stroked his head and slowly moved away, covered him with a sheet and switched off the light. Seeing him sleep like an innocent child, she smiled and realised that however tough and intelligent one may be, one always needs someone during a hard times, because no human is perfect and thus to cover up the faults they have they need another one to be standing with them during their dark and difficult times.

She silently walked away and went to Sihira and Clave and told them that Aiden had fallen asleep and that he had cancelled his travel plan to his former world. At first, Clave doubted her thinking they did not want to take them with them. However, seeing the firmness in Celly's eyes he believed her.

He helped Celly put away the machine in the room, locked it, and went away. The next day, Aiden woke up with dark circles around his eyes and a headache. He felt as if he had been working throughout the night. Celly entered with breakfast and told him freshen up and have his food. Aiden smiled and then stood up and hugged her. She asked him what had happened but he just hugged her without speaking. The image of Celly's death flashed before him repeatedly as he had seen her die many a time a day earlier, it pained him everytime that image flashed in his head and how he was unable to save her.

He went into the bathroom, freshened up, and came out. Celly fed him with her hands. After that, she was about to leave when Aiden asked her what had happened to the machine. She replied that she and Clave had locked it up thinking it would not be of any use anymore. Aiden smiled and told her to take out the machine again as the mission was still on and this time the destination is not Earth-7.

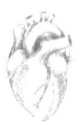

Chapter 19
SECRETS

Aiden told her that when they landed on Earth-7, they had to fear the loop as the curse got activated only after he landed there. The loop began when the curse gets activated. So, instead of landing on Earth-7, they would directly go to the designated location they have discussed at first. Celly asked him why he was so eager to meet him. Aiden replied that he wanted to know why he had suddenly showed up in Dreek even when he was not worshipped there. Why had he placed the source at places easy to find and was the shield really to protect Dreek or was it a gateway or something else like a dangerous trap.

Hearing this, Celly phoned Clave and Sihira to come as soon as possible. When they arrived, they were told of the new plan. Aiden said, "Unless we find him, we shouldn't give up as it may put many people's lives at stake. We need to survive on that unknown planet as we survive on ours. We will start a business of our own on that new planet."

Clave and Sihira were really confused as toi what was going on. They asked him about the business. Aiden smiled and replied, "We still have Karan's stories." Sihira asked if there were humans or other creatures on that planet. Aiden replied, "Karan had talked with Halsifer and according to him there are many planets that have various creatures on them but Earth is the only one where humans and creatures live together. Therefore, it will not be a problem. The last question and the most important one was asked by Celly. It was, "Which planet are we going to land on?" Aiden replied, "Earth-1". Meanwhile Clave had another question that he asked after celly, "Who is this 'he' for whom we are taking such a risk?" Aiden turned to look at him and with a wicked smile replied "The Supreme."

What will Aiden do when he comes face to face with The Supreme? Will he get his answers, or will he face more challenges? Wait and find out in the upcoming books of the multiverse.

THE END
AIDEN AND HIS TEAM WILL RETURN.

======

MORE BOOKS BY THE AUTHOR

www.ingramcontent.com/pod-product-compliance
Lightning Source LLC
LaVergne TN
LVHW061613070526
838199LV00078B/7267